GW00694435

SONG OF THE GUN

All Dakota heard the song of the gun when two range giants declared war on each other.

There was Carse Boling, who ruled the Coffin spread with his fists and his streaking gun hand. There was Sam Jedrow, who rode Coffin out of a past that no man dared to question. They met and they fought, these two savage sons of trouble, over a ranch and a woman that didn't belong to either of them.

Dudley Dean was the name Dudley Dean McGaughey used from the beginning for his series of exemplary Western novels written for Fawcett Gold Medal in the 1950s. McGaughey was born in Rialto, California, and began writing fiction for Street & Smith's Wild West Weekly in the early 1930s under the name Dean Owen. These early stories, and many more longer pulp novels written for Masked Rider Western and Texas Rangers after the Second World War, were aimed at a youthful readership. The 1950s marked McGaughey's Golden Age and virtually all that he wrote as Dudley Dean, Dean Owen, or Lincoln Drew during this decade repays a reader with rich dividends in tense storytelling and historical realism. This new direction can be seen in short novels he wrote early in the decade such as "Gun the Man Down" in *5 Western Novels* (August 1952) and "Hang the Man High!" in *Big-Book Western* (March 1954). They are notable for their maturity and presage the dramatic change in tone and characterization that occur in the first of the Dudley Dean novels, *Ambush At Rincon* (1953). *The Man From Riondo* (1954), if anything, was even better, with considerable scope in terms of locations, variety of characters, and unusual events. *Gun In The Valley* (1957) by Dudley Dean, *Chainlink* (1957) by Owen Evens, and *Rifle Ranch* (1958) by Lincoln Drew are quite probably his finest work among the fine novels from this decade. These stories are notable in particular for the complexity of their social themes and psychological relationships, but are narrated in a simple, straightforward style with such deftly orchestrated plots that their subtlety and depth may become apparent only upon reflection.

SONG OF THE GUN

Dudley Dean

GUNSMOKE

This hardback edition 2003
by Chivers Press
by arrangement with
Golden West Literary Agency

ISBN 0 7540 8226 1

British Library Cataloguing in Publication Data available.

Printed and bound in Great Britain by
Antony Rowe Ltd., Chippenham, Wiltshire

Chapter One

CARSE BOLING rode toward Coffin headquarters and there was no enthusiasm in his going home as there would have been in other years. He rode at the head of the half-dozen men he had taken to inspect, strengthen, and stock the many line shacks of the big ranch before the onslaught of winter. A large man, lean and long-muscled, he pulled up abruptly at sight of two riders approaching through the jack pines, well inside Coffin boundaries.

With unaccustomed harshness he told his men to wait and rode down the slant. One of those approaching was a woman, Allison Kellerway. He was surprised to see her away from the desk in her brother's office in Bellfontaine. He was more surprised to note that she could ride a horse and that the glaring Dakota sun revealed no flaws in her rather interesting face. Neither did she lose her looks in the exchange of shirt and jeans for the prim, starched appearance she gave in town.

The other rider was Ralph Shamley, one of the shirttail beef operators on the other side of Coffin, near the Missouri.

"Hello, Ralph," Carse said when he came up to them. His gaze slid to the girl, who eyed him narrowly out of brown eyes. He wondered then, as he had at each meeting since her arrival in this country, over a month ago, why she so plainly disliked him.

5

"Reckon you know Miss Kellerway," Shamley said.

Carse nodded and the girl said coolly, "We've met."

Carse found the girl's coolness unsettling, and he found release in a controlled anger.

"Ralph, I hope you weren't riding Miss Kellerway clear to Coffin in the hope that she could talk Staggart into selling beef through her brother. We've always sold our beef to Archer. No reason to change packinghouses."

Allison Kellerway's eyes snapped. "Don't flatter yourself, Mr. Boling."

"Ain't no sense in gettin' het up, folks," Shamley said nervously. A bent, gray man, he had aged before his time by trying to compete with big outfits like Coffin and the Radich brothers' Forty-four.

Allison said, "My brother is interested in Shamley's beef."

"Then your brother ought to be looking over Shamley's beef," Carse said. He looked her up and down, over her brown hair, gold at the temples, her tanned throat, the breasts a loose-fitting shirt could not disguise, the long legs that her denims fitted like faded blue skin. "The cattle business is hardly a thing to trust to a woman's judgment," he added.

It pleased him to see her quick anger.

"My brother happens to be out of town," she said icily. "As for not trusting a woman's judgment in cattle, I wish to inform you I know the subject from lifelong experience."

He smiled. She was not more than twenty, if that old. You didn't pick up much knowledge of the cattle business in the short span of her maturity. "Sorry. I didn't realize you were an expert."

Ralph Shamley looked uneasy, and stirred in his saddle. He was caught in the middle. "Guess we strayed a little far over Coffin's line. Didn't realize I was off my own range."

Carse looked at Allison Kellerway and said to Shamley, "*You're* always welcome, Ralph. You know that."

Shamley made an attempt to ease the strain of this animosity that he did not understand between the tall, brown-haired girl and the hard-bitten partner of Staggart at Coffin. "Her brother may option the beef I got ready to ship," Shamley said.

Carse frowned. "Better go easy. Paul Kellerway is a stranger. We don't know much about him."

Allie Kellerway said, "You're hardly in a position to judge my brother's ethics."

Carse considered this, and Shamley moved his horse on down the draw, anxious to have no part in the argument.

"I've got ethics, Miss Kellerway."

Allie said, "Have you now?" There was a trace of angry Irish in her voice.

"Your intense dislike puzzles me."

"Obviously you're an educated man, Mr. Boling. Therefore you should understand without explanation."

"I'm educated after a fashion, but not enough to understand your subtlety."

Her eyes snapped, and she drew back the reins so that her forearm lay across her breasts. "You have a partner—Stag Staggart. He has a young wife. A pretty wife. And you all live under the same roof. Need I say more, Mr. Boling?"

She wheeled her horse and went rocketing past the spot where Shamley waited down the draw. Shamley turned and shrugged expressively to Carse, then spurred after her.

When Shamley finally caught up with her, Allie had slowed her horse to a walk. She was white around the mouth.

Shamley considered Carse Boling his friend and he hoped to point out Carse's good points to this girl.

But she interrupted his explanation. "I don't wish to hear you defend a man who is having an affair with the wife of his partner." When Shamley's mouth hung open in astonishment, Allie, blushing, said, "It's common gossip. I'm surprised Staggart hasn't killed him."

As was his custom, Carse Boling awakened with the first light, hearing Emily Staggart already stirring in the kitchen. He lay a moment to contemplate the luxury of the feather mattress, finding it hard to believe that as Martin Staggart's partner he had spent his last night in this sprawling log house. He rose in the growing day and soberly recalled the meeting with the Kellerway girl late yesterday afternoon. He did not like her little insinuating mind any better than he liked the rest of her.

His eye caught the potted geranium Emily had placed on his window sill. He parted the curtains and looked down at the long yard of Coffin headquarters. Lights glowed in the windows of the bunkhouse, which was large enough to accommodate fifty men comfortably. He could see old Ben Smiley in the doorway of his cook shack, yelling at the roustabouts to hurry with wood for the breakfast fire. Beyond, at the first of the many corrals, he could see a group of men waiting for their names to be put in the time book. Roundup would start in a week and he knew the word was out in Bellfontaine that the second largest spread in the Dakotas was hiring.

He had arrived late last night after his two-week inspection of Coffin line shacks, seeing that the zinc-lined boxes were filled with grub for the winter, checking the roofs. As foreman of so large a spread, he normally would have delegated the job to someone like Johnny D'Orr, Emily's brother. But the growing unpleasantness here had made him decide to make the trip personally. Now that he was back he felt no lessening of the strain between Emily, Staggart, and himself. They had lived here together under this roof since Staggart and Emily had been married, three years ago.

Last night Staggart had only grunted a greeting when Carse rode in.

This morning Carse took a moment to study his reflection in the looking glass Emily had thoughtfully provided. At twenty-nine the lines were not too deep around his wide mouth, but they fanned out on either side of his dark-blue eyes. A shock of black hair fell across a high forehead darkened from the sun and Dakota weather. His nose was prominent and it gave his face a bold look that this morning did not match his feelings. He wondered what it was about his face that Allison Kellerway seemed to find so revolting.

A tall, solid man, he dressed in a clean blue shirt and denim pants, delaying as long as possible the inevitable breakfast in the kitchen. At last he walked along the narrow hall, seeing the strip of light under the kitchen door. The three of them had had something fine together, he reflected soberly.

Staggart was already at the table, his elbows resting on the clean checked tablecloth. Above the kitchen door was Stag's old Sharps rifle, which he always kept loaded.

With false heartiness Carse said, "Mornin'," and threw a leg over a chair. He smiled at Emily, who was frying bacon in a large skillet at the stove.

He noted instantly that Emily's pretty face seemed drawn and the familiar liveliness was gone from her dark eyes. She wore a gingham dress that flared from a tiny waist over her ample hips. She was small, dainty, and well-formed. On her mother's side she was related to half the Oglalas at the Pine Hill Agency. She had woven some Indian beads in the braids of the thick black hair that hung down her slender back. In the house she always wore moccasins. She was twenty years old, and Martin Staggart, who sat watching the way his wife and his foreman regarded each other, had celebrated his forty-first birthday last spring.

Staggart held a tin cup of coffee in his big hands. He had been a large, forceful man, but lately he seemed to have acquired an inner softness that Carse could not understand. Staggart's brown hair was shaggy, as was his mustache.

They talked a moment about range conditions, but Carse sensed that Staggart was not interested. Staggart kept glancing at Emily. Then he would give Carse an odd, calculating look. Staggart's pale eyes were bloodshot and were circled darkly. Carse knew his partner had drunk himself to sleep again.

"You done any more thinking about our problem?" Staggart said.

"A little."

Carse drank the coffee Emily set before him. There was the clean woman smell of her that he had missed during his two weeks away from the home ranch. He was aware of a queer, twisting sensation in the pit of his stomach when he saw the startling whiteness of her teeth in the brief and helpless smile she gave him behind her husband's back. The smile said, Since you've been gone nothing has changed. My husband is a jealous man.

Staggart said, "Margretha gets in on the train today."

The warm feeling Carse had experienced a moment before at Emily's presence died, and he knew the subject of Staggart's niece would have to be faced. He was aware of a tension as he met Emily's eyes.

Staggart took the skillet from his wife and poured bacon drippings over the corn bread he had crumbled on his plate. "You thought any more about our talk?" he asked.

"Margretha ought to have some say about who she marries," Carse said.

"You put a ring on her finger and it'll make it pretty good for you, Carse."

Carse clenched his teeth. "You haven't seen her since she was a kid. How do you know she wants to come to this Godforsaken place to get herself a husband?"

"Every woman wants a husband," Staggart said, and gave his wife an oblique look. "Ain't that right, Em?"

Emily brushed a tendril of black hair from her damp forehead. "I suppose so."

Again, as he had two weeks ago, Martin Staggart laid a photograph and a letter on the table.

The letter said: "Uncle Martin: I've intended to write since Mamma died. It's been so long since I've seen you I think it might be nice if I visited you for the winter. . . ."

There was more to Margretha Lenrick's letter, but Carse did not bother to read it. With a thick forefinger he turned the photograph around and studied it. She was a pale, pretty girl. Refined, from good stock, Staggart had told him.

He tried to make his voice light as he said, "Am I obligated to marry your niece just because I'm your partner and foreman?"

Staggart's eyes were hard under bushy brows as he studied the younger man's face. "You own twenty per cent of Coffin," the rancher reminded Carse. "And you draw foreman's pay. For a fella still under thirty, you done pretty well. Now just because I ask you to think about marrying my niece, you—"

Carse felt the back of his neck getting warm. He saw Emily standing helplessly by the woodbox, her small hands tightly clenched.

"I've worked for what I have," Carse reminded Stag. He could have reminded the man of other things, such as the day seven years ago when Carse Boling had headed into the Dakotas with a small herd of Texas cattle and found Staggart unconscious and bleeding to death from a bad thigh wound. Staggart had jumped some horse thieves alone and they had shot him and left him to die. Carse had saved his life and the two of them had formed a partnership, and together they had saved the tottering Coffin from foreclosure. Others in the Dakotas were not so fortunate. Many people expected the boom following the Civil War to continue for another ten years. When it didn't, a lot of the big outfits went under.

Emily put bacon and beans on Carse's plate, then sat down to eat her own breakfast. When her husband persisted in his talk about his niece, Emily said, "I think it's up to Carse whether he wants to marry her or not."

"Maybe you wouldn't like it," Staggart said coldly, "if Carse had a wife."

Carse felt a swift rage. "Yesterday the sister of that two-bit cattle buyer, Paul Kellerway, hinted there was something between Emily and me. Now what the hell's going on, Stag?"

Staggart scowled at the plate of grease-soaked corn bread. "Well, anyhow, it would stop the talk if you had a wife."

"Who's been spreading talk about Emily and me?" Carse demanded again.

Staggart thumbed a shaggy brow and Carse could see the belligerence grow in the man, as it always did when he was cornered.

"I just figure Carse might want a wife," he said, scowling at Emily. "Is there anything wrong in that?"

Emily said, "I can tell you the day everything changed at Coffin. It was the day a month ago you hired Sam Jedrow to break horses."

Chapter Two

CARSE STUDIED Emily's face, wondering why she considered Sam Jedrow responsible for the change in their lives. There was a tight silence in the kitchen, broken only by the crackle of wood in the firebox of the big range. From the dining room adjoining the cook shack across the yard he could hear the muted clamor of the thirty-odd Coffin hands trooping in for the morning meal. He knew that in the future he would be taking his meals with the men, for Margretha would move into his quarters here in the house. No matter what might happen, he thought soberly, things would never again be quite the same.

Emily said angrily, "Stag, you've always been a man who spoke his mind. Suddenly you're evasive; you drink too much." She leaned forward, her slender hands locked at the edge of the table. "I'm beginning to wonder if this Sam Jedrow isn't something ugly from your past."

Color drained from Staggart's face. Carse was shocked to see Staggart slump back in his chair and stare at the ceiling. There was a decided change in the man. He no longer seemed the brazen stockman Carse remembered. Carse knew little about the man other than the fact that Staggart had come to Dakota a decade ago. No one seemed to know where he had come from or what his past life might have been. And Carse sensed that Emily had learned nothing more in the three years she had been mistress of Coffin. Originally Staggart's brand had been a B Box B. Once a drummer had remarked that it looked like a coffin, an oblong box with the B at both ends forming the handles. The name had stuck.

Carse had no appetite and he rolled a cigarette. He felt sorry for Emily. Her life had not been easy in this country, which showed little tolerance for her or her brother, Johnny. Even though their father had been French-Canadian, they were classed by many as Indians.

Carse said, "I never liked Jedrow. And it's the first time you ever took on a man without consulting me."

Staggart said gruffly, "We need horses for the *remuda*. Roundup's almost here."

12

"I'd like to know how many horses he's broken since he's been on the payroll. Or doesn't it matter because maybe he's a special friend you knew somewhere before you came to Dakota?"

Staggart rose abruptly from the table and jerked his hat from an elk-horn rack beneath the pegs that held the big .50-caliber Sharps rifle. "Margretha Lenrick is the only kin I got in the world," Staggart said. "If you and her was to marry, you'd be a full-fledged partner of mine."

Carse stared through the window to the yard, where daylight erased shadows and brought out the faces of the men waiting at the corral to be hired for roundup. "I hoped one day to buy more of an interest in Coffin," he said. "I didn't plan to marry it."

"That ain't the way I meant it at all," Staggart protested. "But think it over. Can't you do that much for me?"

The kitchen door slammed as Staggart went out.

Emily said, "He's talked of nothing else since the day his niece's letter arrived. He's intent on having you marry the girl."

Carse sat on the edge of the table and took one of her small hands in his. "Em, would it make things easier for you if I got Stag to buy me out?"

He saw a flush steal over her pretty face. "Your being here is the only thing that's made it bearable." Her eyes were pleading. "Don't go, Carse." Then, embarrassed, she rose and hurried into the back part of the house.

Troubled, he stepped into the yard and caught sight of Staggart beside the kitchen door. "It isn't like you to eavesdrop," Carse told his partner stiffly.

He started for the cook shack where the regular hands were waiting for their assignments. The drifters by the corral saw him coming and straightened up, and some of them threw aside their cigarettes and brushed dust from their clothing. They would work the roundup and then be turned loose to drift until spring touched this land again. Suddenly he hated the Dakotas and Coffin and Staggart; this narrow insular world where he was forced to live.

He heard Staggart's low-voiced plea and turned as Staggart came up and said, "Carse, don't pay no mind to me. I—"

"Maybe I ought to pull out, Stag."

"I need you now, Carse," he said softly, "a hell of a

lot more than I did seven years ago when you found me bleedin' to death."

Carse was touched by the urgency in his partner's voice. "Stag, something's eating you."

The evasiveness Emily had mentioned colored Staggart's voice. "Meet Margretha today in Bellfontaine. If you and her hit it off—"

"You're set on me taking a wife so it'll stop gossip. That's it, isn't it, Stag?"

He saw the firming of Staggart's mouth below the mustache. He knew all too well Staggart's jealous nature. In town Stag would watch Emily to see if she glanced at another man. Once a drummer helped Emily across a muddy street, and if Carse hadn't interfered, Stag would have knocked the man down.

Stag said, "Marry my niece and you'll get fifty per cent of Coffin the day you put a ring on her finger."

Carse said, "It's Jedrow that's been doing the talking about Emily and me. Why? And if he's got something on you, for God's sake, speak up."

Staggart looked down at the toes of his worn boots. "I'm asking you one thing: Stay with me through round-up. After that things will be like they always was."

"Things will be the same? How?"

"Jedrow will be gone from here."

At that moment Sam Jedrow came out of the bunkhouse and crossed to them, the sharpened rowels of his Chihuahua spurs raking up a small cloud of dust. He was an immense man, thick and tall, and wearing a flat-crowned hat that seemed incongruous on his massive skull. Without shoes he would stand a good five inches over six feet. Jedrow gave Carse a quick look out of cold green eyes, then addressed himself to Staggart.

"Like to have a talk with you, Stag," the big bronc buster said, "when you're alone."

Staggart, who usually resented a new man's calling him by his nickname, nodded and said to Carse, "See you when you get back from meeting the train."

As Carse moved to the cook shack he felt that the masonry of his well-ordered existence was beginning to show cracks. A deep fear had leavened the familiar bluster in Staggart; fear and his natural jealousy, which for some reason had been directed at Carse.

Carse gave orders to have a wagon made ready, then entered the cook shack, where roustabouts were cleaning up after the morning meal. For the first time he felt almost like an intruder on this ranch that had been his home for seven years. For the second time in his life he felt unsure of his position; the first time had been in Texas, with a girl named Della.

He turned and looked across the yard. Staggart and Jedrow were engaged in animated conversation in the shade of the big log house.

Old Ben Smiley, wiping his hands on a greasy apron, came to stand at his side. He nodded at Jedrow. "Big fella, ain't he, Carse?"

Carse made no comment, but told the old cook he was going to town. "Give me your list and I'll bring out the stuff you need for roundup."

From a torn shirt pocket Smiley removed a list. He was a bald little man with a bowed right leg. His left leg was crooked, the result of a roundup accident years ago. "Carse, I—" The old man seemed embarrassed. "Well, I just can't figure that Jedrow. He's drawing bronc-buster pay, but do you know he ain't busted one horse in the month he's been here?"

Carse shrugged. "Anything else on your mind, Ben?"

Ben Smiley's narrow lined face was flushed. "Since you been gone there's been some talk about Emily Staggart. I thought you ought to know." Ben Smiley stepped back as if to avoid the anger that crossed Carse Boling's dark face. "I ain't sayin' it's true or where I heard it," Ben Smiley went on, "but I figure—"

"Then why are you telling me?"

"I figured you oughta know that Johnny's takin' it to heart. You know that boy's temper, and he's made some talk that if he hears any more insults about his sister—"

Carse put a hand on the old man's thin arm. "You leave Johnny to me. Thanks anyhow, Ben."

Ben Smiley said worriedly, "I got a feeling Jedrow is deliberately baiting the boy."

Carse went out into the yard and crossed to the bunkhouse. He found a solitary figure there. Emily's brother sat on a bunk using a cleaning rag on a Colt .45. Johnny looked up, his dark face smiling briefly. He asked Carse how the trip to the line shacks had been.

Carse said things were in good shape. He watched Johnny load the revolver. He knew of Johnny's weaknesses, of his resentment when he was the butt of jokes in Bellfontaine. "Watch out that Injun don't lift your scalp," they'd say. "Hey, Johnny, why ain't you cut out the seat of your britches like your Oglala cousins do at Pine Hills Reservation?"

Johnny was five years younger than Carse, but they were good friends. Older than Emily, he did not have his sister's stability. It had been Emily's great fear, she had confided once to Carse, that as Johnny grew older he would allow his bitterness to flare into violence.

Carse remarked about the early hour Johnny had chosen for cleaning his Colt.

"Rattlesnakes got a habit of getting out early," Johnny said, his black Indian eyes on Carse's face. "If a man plans to shoot one, he should have a clean gun."

Carse knew better than to accuse Johnny directly of planning to use the gun against a man. Johnny was smart, educated, but there was enough Indian in him to make him stubborn and sometimes suspicious of even his best friend's motives. The father of Emily and Johnny had come to this country from Canada to teach school. But there had been no one to teach. Late in life he had lived with the Oglalas and married a chief's daughter. When his wife died and the town of Bellfontaine was founded, he had returned to Dakota and taught school until his death. He had lived just long enough to see his daughter married and his son with a lifetime job at Coffin.

Suddenly Carse Boling made up his mind to take the easy way out of the situation in which he had become involved. A man had to look out for his own interests. He now had a 20-per-cent interest in the ranch. This morning Staggart had pointed out how he could have more.

Carse said lightly, "Will you dance at my wedding?"

Johnny finished loading the gun. "You'll never marry."

"A man can change his mind."

Johnny D'Orr shook his dark head. "You could have married the Adams girl or that redheaded widow, or you could have married—" Johnny broke off abruptly.

Carse told him about Stag's niece. "If I marry her I'll have a full half interest." He laughed about it, but somehow it left a bad taste in his mouth.

Johnny said, "You don't even know the girl."

"I've seen her picture. It's enough for men who take themselves a picture bride. Why not me?"

Johnny said, "One thing for sure. Emily won't dance at your wedding."

Something in Johnny's tone caused Carse to turn and stare the length of the big bunkhouse. "Why'd you say that, Johnny?"

Johnny D'Orr tossed the gun on his bunk and stood up. "Emily's been in love with you for years."

Carse looked at him. There was more Indian in Johnny's features than in Emily's. "She picked Stag," Carse reminded him bluntly. "He's been a good husband."

"Good husband," Johnny said through his teeth. "I promised Papa I'd watch out for Emily. I aim to." Johnny could never keep his dislike for Staggart from showing.

A step at the far end of the bunkhouse caused them to look around. Sam Jedrow came along the line of bunks, his Chihuahua spurs chiming. From beneath his bunk, near the door, he withdrew a small cowhide trunk and unlocked it. He took out a black suit and white shirt.

"Wonder if he overheard us talking," Carse said softly.

Johnny said, "Emily's got a stake in Coffin. I won't stand by and see her robbed of it." He was glaring at Jedrow, who had removed his work shirt and exposed his broad back to them.

Carse said, "You let me handle Jedrow."

He moved to the door and Jedrow saw him, apparently for the first time. Their eyes met. Jedrow said, "I got a couple of friends who want to hire on for roundup." His forehead was scarred. His nose might once have been beaked, but now it was shapeless in the center of his broad face, as if it had been flattened by a fist or the sole of a boot.

"Staggart does the hiring these days," Carse said thinly.

Jedrow smiled and Carse could see the strong white teeth. "These friends of mine are good hands." He turned deliberately and peered the length of the shadowed building at Johnny D'Orr. "But they might not like havin' to bunk with a damn Indian any more than I do."

Carse had started to move on, but now he spun. From a corner of his eye he saw Johnny D'Orr reaching for the .45 on his bunk. He cried, "Johnny, hold it!"

When Johnny froze, Carse said, "Don't ever let me hear you say that again, Jedrow." Carse was a tall man, but because of Jedrow's height he was forced to peer up at him. "You remember."

"Sure—boss." Jedrow resumed changing his clothes.

Carse jerked his head and Johnny followed him into the yard. "He's trying to pick a fight with you," Carse warned. "Stay away from him."

"The bastard," Johnny said, and spat through his teeth.

"Remember this, Johnny. We'll be here a long time after Jedrow's gone." And he wondered then if he really believed it himself. "Roundup is next week. Let's play it easy till we ship beef. With that out of the way, we'll find out about Jedrow. Who he is and why he's here and why Stag is scared sick of him."

When Johnny finally agreed to stay away from the big bronc buster, Carse hunted up Staggart. Stag was hiring on the extra crew for roundup. Carse got him aside and told him of his decision.

"If your niece will look twice at me, I think you'll have me in the family."

Some of the tension seemed to leave Staggart's face. "I'm mighty glad to hear that, Carse. It'll make things easier all around. We'll build you and Margretha a house yonderly." He flung out a hand, indicating a knoll covered with jack pine some distance away.

Carse said, "I guess it saves talk if a man and wife live together under their own roof."

Staggart looked worried again. "Don't be sore, Carse. I don't believe them stories about you and Em."

Carse went to the wagon that had been made ready for him. One of the young roustabouts, Hank Peavey, said, "Ben Smiley figures you'll need help loading the wagon in town."

Carse started to tell him he could handle the wagon himself. Then he thought it might be better if he had someone along on the ride back with Margretha. For some reason he didn't want to be alone with the girl. Not yet. He told Peavey to come along.

Peavey was thin, with a large Adam's apple, big gray eyes, and a shock of tawny hair. He was strong and Ben Smiley said that Hank would one day make a top hand. He was nineteen.

Carse drove the team rapidly past the big log house, the barns, and the corrals, and then along the road that would lead to the Missouri River and Bellfontaine.

Hank Peavey said, "I hear this fella Paul Kellerway is goin' to line up all the little outfits hereabouts. He claims he can get more money for their beef if they sell through him."

"They better find out about Kellerway before they go signing with him," Carse remarked. "Nobody ever heard of him."

"He's sure got a good-lookin' sister, though."

"I hadn't noticed."

"You sure must be blind, Carse. I mean Mr. Boling."

Carse laughed. "Nobody calls me Mr. Boling except people I don't like."

"Sure, Carse. But this Allison Kellerway—they call her Allie—is sure a looker. I swear they say the little outfits is signin' up only because she rides out and talks it over with them and sits a horse like a man. Some of the womenfolks say she's brazen—that if a woman wants to ride a horse she should be a lady and do it sidesaddle. Just seein' her on that horse with them tight-fittin' britches makes me itch." He explored the subject further.

"Hank, have you ever had a woman?"

Hank Peavey blushed. "No."

"A fella don't talk so much about it once he's had one."

Chapter Three

HARDLY HAD CARSE driven out of the yard than Jedrow came from the bunkhouse to stand beside Staggart. "Seems to be in a hurry," he observed, and pointed at the racing wagon.

"It's a time for hurry. He's goin' to meet a girl. Maybe marry her."

Jedrow wore his black suit. "Don't blame you for tryin' to marry him off. He's a good-lookin' fella. If I had a pretty wife and him livin' in the same house, I'd sure watch to see she didn't walk in her sleep."

A purple vein stood out on Staggart's forehead. "Damn you, Sam. I trust Emily. I trust Carse." He cursed. "I watched 'em this mornin' in the kitchen. If they was guilty it'd show on their faces. Now I want you to quit that talk, you understand?"

Jedrow spread his big hands. "The talk didn't start with me. I told you that. Somebody seen 'em off in the woods together. Cozy, they was, so I hear."

"By God, if I had the guts of a worm I'd have my crew kick you off this place!"

Jedrow seemed not to have heard. He was staring at the cloud of dust kicked up by Carse Boling's wagon, lying in a yellow cloud against the low hills. "Stag, did I ever tell you about the time I was deputy at Mogollon? Well, I take this fella out of jail just as the sun is comin' up. And this fella is so scared I got to pick him up and carry him to the gallows."

Staggart nervously brushed a hand across his thick mustache. "Stop it, Sam. Stop it!"

"I put the noose around his neck. It must do something to a man's pride to be hanged in front of a big crowd. Undignified, they call it. You know, Stag, some of the folks were laughin'. There was women and kids in the crowd, and this fella's wife was there. When I let him drop through the trap she began screaming. I can hear her yet."

Staggart lurched across the yard and into the house.

In a moment Emily Staggart came to the yard, her face

pale. She crossed determinedly to where Jedrow still stood. The part in her hair was clean and straight. There was Indian anger in her dark eyes. "What did you just say to my husband to upset him so?" she demanded of Jedrow.

Slowly Jedrow removed his hat and his big face softened a little. "I didn't say nothin', ma'am."

"You frightened him. Why? Why are you here? Why are you doing these things to my husband?"

The arrogance, the brutality left Jedrow's eyes. "It's one of the things I don't like, ma'am—you bein' here. I don't like it at all."

Her mouth slowly opened and she watched him cross the yard to a saddle horse. She saw him spur the horse cruelly along the road to town.

Puzzled and a little frightened, she returned to the house. If only she could confide in Carse. She thought of the years she had clerked in Si Gorman's store in Bellfontaine. She remembered how she would look forward to Carse Boling's visits to the store. She would feel flushed and fumbling when she took his order. She waited long and hopefully, and finally Staggart asked for her hand.

She found Staggart lying on the parlor sofa, drinking from a whisky bottle.

"Please, Stag, tell me what's troubling you."

He took another drink and the whisky fired his anger so that it quelled the great fright that had shaken him. He stared at her out of his pale eyes. A big, shaggy man, he tried to bluster, but it did not hide his fear. "You ask me what's the matter!" he cried, the whisky making his tongue reckless. "You and Carse was seen last year when I went with the beef train to Chi. Out in the woods you was seen. Cozy, you was."

She said, "Now I know what you really think of me."

When she turned to leave the room he lunged from the sofa and caught her by the arm. "Tell me it ain't true!"

She looked at him, trembling. "Turn me loose!" she ordered, and tried to pry his fingers from her arm.

"By God, it *is* true!"

She bared her white teeth. "It was last fall when you went to Chicago. Has it taken you all this time to learn that your wife is a slut?"

Her words shocked him. "I ought to—"

She tried to hide her fear of him with laughter. "While you're thinking of what to do with me, maybe you can explain what you do every year in Bellfontaine after the shipping is over."

Her attack startled him and he grew wary. "I spend a week playin' poker, drinkin' with the fellas."

"Next time I see Oren Goodfellow on the street I'm going to ask him when he started selling lip paint with his whisky at the saloon. Lip paint that you can smear on your neck and on the front of your shirt. While you're thinking that over, I'll answer your question. I've never in my life been with another man. I'm surprised you would even ask."

She jerked her hand from his grasp and fled to the bedroom, where she flung herself across the bed and sobbed wildly.

Staggart stood stunned for a moment, and then he saw that Johnny D'Orr had come quietly to stand in the kitchen doorway. "Next time keep your voice down," Johnny said. "Either that or leave my sister alone. Because if I ever come in here and find you putting a hand on her again, I'll kill you."

For a full quarter of a minute Staggart looked at his brother-in-law. Then with a cry of rage he snatched a kerosene lamp with a hand-painted shade from a table. He hurled it at Johnny, but the man had gone. The lamp crashed against the wall and in a moment there was the pungent odor of spilled kerosene.

Staggart picked up the bottle he had left on the sofa. He drew the cork with his teeth and spat it into the fireplace. Then he stood erect until he had drained the bottle. Only then did he collapse across the sofa.

Presently Emily came and looked at the shattered lamp and at her husband. In a minute she drew off her husband's boots and pulled his dangling feet up on the sofa. Then she went to clean up the kerosene.

Carse drove the wagon through the Dakota heat. Hank Peavey clung to the seat brace and talked of someday maybe having a spread like Coffin. "You sure got a nice setup, Carse."

Carse shrugged. "Depends on how you look at it. I had a lot of luck."

The road crossed the rim of a deep draw and then went down the other side. As the wagon jolted, the Winchester in the scabbard lashed to the seat rattled against the brake handle.

At the bottom of the grade was a water hole, and Carse pulled up and watered the team. He rolled a cigarette, sniffing the air for the first smell of the Missouri. In the distance, through a fringe of cottonwoods, he could see the buildings of Ralph Shamley's Anchor spread. He wondered grimly how Ralph had made out with the Kellerway girl, and if the rancher was fool enough to option cattle to a man he didn't know.

He and Peavey were on the ground, stretching. When the horses had drunk their fill, Carse started to climb to the seat. Hank Peavey said, "Mind if I drive?"

"Go ahead."

In the moment it took to shift the reins from one pair of hands to the other there was a dull flat sound. It was followed an instant later by the crashing of a heavy gun. Hank Peavey spun and fell against the wagon and tried to claw at the sideboards. The team, frightened, started running, and Carse vainly tried to grab the reins. Failing, he managed to jerk the Winchester from its scabbard as the wagon flashed by. He shot a glance at Peavey, lying face down in the road. Peavey was dead.

Then he levered in a shell and fired again and again up the slope toward a faint curling of black powder among the jack pines.

"You son-of-a-bitch!" he cried at the trees and the smudge of powder. He emptied the rifle and scrambled up the slope, reloading. He slipped on gravel, picked himself up. There was no sign of an ejected shell when he reached a small clearing and found tracks of horse and man. Far in the distance he could hear the sounds of a hard-running horse. He could see where his own bullets had slashed the tree trunks.

As he ran back to the road he cursed the bolted team. He had no horse with which to ride in pursuit of the ambusher. He levered Peavey over on his back and felt his stomach lurch. The bullet had struck Peavey high on the left shoulder, been deflected by bone, and coursed downward to tear a gaping hole just above the belt buckle.

Carse pulled the body into the meager shade of a boulder beside the water hole. Then, rifle in hand, he went in search of the team and wagon. He knew there had been one rider up there on the slope and that the man had ridden east. Although he saw no blood on the ground at the spot where the ambusher had lurked, Carse fervently hoped he had winged the man. It was an hour before he found the team and wagon. An indentation in the wagon sideboard caught his attention. With the blade of his clasp knife he dug out a large chunk of flattened lead. He knew this was the bullet that had torn through Peavey.

When he returned to the water hole he saw Ralph Shamley and two of his riders coming down the slant. The gray, bent rancher gave an exclamation of surprise when he saw the body. His two riders dismounted with him. They were weathered men, their clothing worn.

"The Peavey kid," one of them said.

Shamley knelt beside the body. "We heard some shots an hour or so ago, Carse. Guess this was it. What happened?"

"We finished watering the team. Hank wanted to drive. I changed places with him and he got the bullet."

Shamley got slowly to his feet. "That shot was meant for you?" he asked incredulously.

Carse nodded. He asked if they had seen anyone prowling about, but they had seen no one. "It's a little late to go after him now," Carse said. "He's likely across the river. But he'll try again. Next time I'll get him."

"Who you reckon it was, Carse?" Shamley asked.

"I can only guess."

"I hear the Radich brothers are getting big ideas," Shamley said. "You reckon one of their boys did this?"

"Bert and his brother play a tough game," Carse said. "They don't go in for bushwhacking." He removed the chunk of lead from his pocket. "This is what did it. From a Sharps, wouldn't you say, Ralph?"

Shamley examined the lead. "Yeah, a Sharps."

"Not many fellas carry a gun that big any more. Not since most of the buffalo are gone." Carse boarded the wagon. "I got to get to town. Will you see that Hank is taken to Coffin? I'd appreciate it, Ralph."

When he drove off, one of Shamley's men remarked, "He's a coldhearted son. Don't give a damn that the kid died so he could live."

"You don't know Carse," Shamley said. "He don't show his feelin's much. He's tore all to hell inside."

They started to roll the body in a slicker. "Say, ain't Staggart got a Sharps rifle? Be something if them stories about Carse and Emily Staggart are true. Maybe Stag figured to do a little hunting today with his Sharps."

Carse drove on a mile or so. Then he braked the wagon and smoked two cigarettes. An hour later he was crossing the Missouri River on Merle Lanniman's ferry. The old ferryman squinted at Carse. "Your eyes are red. You look like you been cryin'."

"It's the dust. If we don't get some rain in this country it'll blow away in the first wind."

Carse swung down from the wagon and looked at the broad Missouri. He stood at the town of Bellfontaine on the eastern bank. "Oh, God," he whispered, "and the poor kid didn't even live long enough to get himself a woman."

Chapter Four

As Merle Lanniman steered his ferry across the Missouri, he remarked that Sam Jedrow had crossed over two hours ago.

Carse stiffened, turning from the swirling water that piled against the cumbersome craft. "Was he carrying a Sharps?"

"Didn't have no gun that I could see." Lanniman was small and possessed of a shrewd eye. "Why you ask?" When Carse made no reply, he went on: "Jedrow says Staggart's niece is comin' here to live. Guess Stag wants the girl to keep an eye on Mrs. Staggart. To see that she don't stray."

Carse turned on him. "Merle, if you were a younger man I'd dump you in the river."

Lanniman said, chuckling, "Some advantages in bein' an old man, at that." Then he gave Carse a shrewd glance. "Jedrow sure is a big man. I'd hate to tangle with him. I've heard he can cripple a man with them spurs he wears. You watch out for him, Carse. He seems to think you and him will have trouble before long."

"Shouldn't wonder," Carse said. "But he'll never get close enough to use those spurs on me. Not as long as I can shoot a gun."

Carse drove the wagon into Bellfontaine, which most of the year was a somnolent town. Then for six weeks, when beef was driven in from the west and loaded into the long strings of cattle cars destined for eastern markets, Bellfontaine took on the appearance of a small, noisy city. Here was the end of track, where the trails and the wagon roads of the vast land of Dakota and the farther wilderness converged. A river packet's whistle hooted as Carse moved along Chicago Street. The deadness of the town and all that had happened this day depressed him. It was a hell of a country to live in, he reflected, and found himself longing for the Texas he had cursed in his youth.

Now the arid borderland took on a new dimension from his long absence. He forgot the heat and the ticks and the Comanches, remembering only the good things. Caught up in nostalgia, he wondered if Della had changed in seven years and if she still had the ring he had not bothered to take back from her. He could hardly remember how she looked, but he could still remember the shock he had felt that day when he had come home unexpectedly from a cattle-selling trip. He never did learn the name of the man he found in her room at the boardinghouse. But he had wanted to kill him. He was glad now he hadn't resorted to violence. Carse sold the small ranch he had run with his father and drove some of the herd north to the Dakotas. A dark suspicion of the motives of women had burgeoned in him during the passing years. Only Emily Staggart seemed genuine. Many times he had considered Staggart to be the most fortunate man in the world.

A husky, good-humored voice hailed him. He pulled up in front of a two-story building with shuttered windows and a bright-red door. Big Min was on the porch of her establishment, stirring the dust-laden air across her moist plump face with a Japanese fan. She weighed three hundred pounds and claimed there was never a corset built that would hold her in. She would say, "What the hell, let the body sag. Nobody comes to see me, anyhow."

"What day's Coffin going to ship this year?" Min called as she waddled down the porch steps.

"Hard to say, Min." Carse waited, knowing this big woman with the humorous eyes and the bleached hair had more on her mind than the Coffin shipping date.

"I s'pose Stag will be staying a week at my place, as usual," Min said.

"I s'pose," Carse said, and as usual found it hard to justify Stag's straying from Emily.

"Sometimes when Stag gets drunk he talks a lot," Min said in a confidential tone of voice. "I just want you to know that what he says here don't go no farther. And that goes for anybody who works for me."

Carse had a certain respect for Min. Any grub-line rider down on his luck who wasn't too proud to knock on her door would get a stake if she considered him worthy of her charity. When Merle Lanniman's wife was dying, it was Min that put her on a train and sent her to the best hospital in Chicago. Afterward the ferryboat operator vehemently denied that he had accepted help from anyone like Big Min, but Carse knew the truth.

"Has somebody been asking questions about Stag?"

"I stay on my side of the fence, Carse. I got to in my business." She looked up and down the nearly deserted street. "Reckon Stag's got something on his mind. Pulling the cork in here once a year helps him get rid of it." She gave Carse an odd smile. "A man's got to get rid of the pressure somehow. I seen it done another way. A man putting the muzzle of a revolver against the roof of his mouth."

"I guess Stag's way is the best." He looked at the two-story building with its shuttered windows. From inside came the sounds of someone practicing the piano. "Funny about life, Min. I figured to have a talk with you today. Know the Peavey boy?"

Min frowned. "Can't say I do, Carse."

"He worked for Coffin. Just a boy. I figured he was ripe to make himself a man. So I thought maybe you'd sort of make the transition a little easier."

"Too bad there aren't a few nice girls in a town like this. A boy gets mighty lonely." She shrugged. "I s'pose a boy's goin' to become a man sometimes and it's best to see he don't get sick. You send him around, Carse."

"That's what I mean about life being funny, Min. Not funny in the sense you want to laugh. Funny in the sense that it's so goddamn tragic it makes a man wonder if there's any purpose in it at all."

"What are you trying to say, Carse?"

"Hank Peavey was shot to death this morning."

"That poor kid. How awful!" Min's face paled. "Oh, God, Carse, I hope this ain't the start of trouble. I went through hell once when I had a place where two big outfits started shootin' each other up."

"What made you mention two big outfits, Min?"

"Coffin and the Radich brothers' Forty-four are the two big ones in this country."

Carse said, "You heard any talk, Min?"

Min's eyes were veiled. "I hear Bert Radich don't like it because Paul Kellerway is lining up the small ranchers."

"That's not my problem. I never liked Bert much. But if he killed Hank Peavey for some reason or other, or ordered it done, I'll settle with him."

"The thing that puzzles me, Carse, is why anybody would want to shoot a kid."

"He just happened to change places with me at the last minute."

Min's mouth hung open. "You watch yourself, Carse. I got a nose for trouble, and it's been twitching overtime the last few weeks."

In Paul Kellerway's office, above Si Gorman's store, Jedrow sat with his body wedged tightly in an armchair. On the window was a sign: "Paul Kellerway, Dealer in Livestock, Representing Fairchild & Morse, Chicago."

Paul Kellerway was in his middle thirties, a lean, handsome man, graying at the temples. He wore a well-cut suit and a white shirt. His fingers nervously tapped the edge of the flat-topped desk.

Jedrow scowled blackly at Kellerway's handsome face. "The only thing I don't like is the talk about Mrs. Staggart."

Kellerway frowned and peered from the window into the street, where a freight wagon lumbered along the alley beside Oren Goodfellow's saloon. "The talk is a necessary part of the plan, Sam. I thought I explained that."

Jedrow picked at his nails. "Is the talk true?"

Kellerway looked irritated. "Why is that important?"

"I want to know if Emily Staggart and Carse Boling was really seen together." Jedrow sat forward, big hands gripping the arms of his chair. "Did you run into somebody who really saw them together like you claim?"

Kellerway laughed. "So far as I know, the story is a falsehood. I dropped a few dollars in the right places. There are always men who will tell the right sort of story for a drink or a dollar."

Jedrow settled back in his chair, but the black expression did not leave his heavy face. "Just thinkin' about the story that's been goin' around almost made me put a bullet in Carse Boling this morning."

"You will eventually," Kellerway said. Then he leaned across the desk. "Don't tell me you're sick of the scheme."

"I just don't like the talk going around about the Staggart woman."

"Well, it's vital. I believe it will stir up trouble between Staggart and Boling. At the last minute Staggart might develop some guts. Although we can still pressure him, it might simplify things if his mind is on his wife's conduct instead of on us. Understand?"

"I still don't like dragging a fine woman like Emily Staggart into the mud."

Kellerway looked at him in surprise. "It's the first time I ever knew you to show a conscience, Sam."

The big, scowling man said, "She reminds me of Lydia."

Kellerway pursed his lips. "She does, at that, now that you mentioned it. I never thought of it before." He rose and said, "Just don't make the mistake of falling for Mrs. Staggart. But you've got more sense than that, eh, Sam?"

Sam Jedrow lumbered out of the office without replying.

Chapter Five

CARSE GAVE the order Ben Smiley had written out to Si Gorman. The little balding storekeeper hurried to fill it. Carse helped himself to a cracker from the barrel. He remembered the first time he had seen Emily behind the counter, small and dark and smiling at him. And that night Stag had said, "By God, I aim to marry that girl one day, if she'll have me."

Carse watched Gorman going over the list and said casually that he might be taking himself a bride. Gorman seemed surprised, but only for a minute. "Can't figure you'd change that much, Carse. Plenty of women around here figured you was going to marry 'em. Sarah Adams and that handsome red-haired widow . . ." He chuckled and gave Carse an old man's envious smile. "But like the fella says, no use putting a ring in the cow's nose if she'll lay down for you without it."

There was a sudden vigorous clearing of a female throat and both men turned to see the tall, shapely Allison Kellerway step into view from where she had been hidden behind a stack of tinned goods.

Gorman said, "I'm right sorry, Miss Kellerway. I didn't see you come in."

Instead of her range garb, she wore today a flowered dress of some thin material that clung to her. And Carse was reminded of what Hank Peavey had said of this girl he had seen riding in a pair of denims. "Seein' her in them britches makes me itch."

Allie Kellerway, seeing the sudden change in his dark-blue eyes, mistook it for anger. "I'm very sorry," she snapped, "if I interrupted the discussion of your many conquests, Mr. Boling. But it so happens I'd like to have Mr. Gorman show me some yard goods."

Gorman looked pained while Allie surveyed Carse Boling coolly from his dusty boots to the hat he wore cuffed back on his black hair. "Instead of bragging of your romances," she said in that icy voice, "I should think you'd be ashamed. At least of the ugly talk that concerns you and Emily Staggart."

31

Carse stood rigid and Si Gorman nervously coughed behind his hand. Carse gripped her arm. "If there's one thing I detest, it's a gossipy female," he said. "Emily Staggart is a fine woman. Do you understand that?"

Allie said, "You're hurting me." She ran the tip of her tongue over her lower lip.

There was a footstep and Carse looked over his shoulder to see that Paul Kellerway had entered the store and was threading his way through the counters. Carse had been introduced to him a month ago, when Kellerway had opened his office here as a representative for what was supposed to be a big Chicago packing house, Fairchild and Morse. As far as Carse knew, no one had ever heard of the firm before.

Carse removed his hand from Allie's arm. She was peering at him, rubbing her arm, an odd look in her eyes. Her brother, coming up, swung his gaze from his sister to Carse. The smile he usually wore tightened a little.

He put out his hand and Carse was forced to shake it. Kellerway wore a neatly trimmed mustache; there was talc on his cheeks. "Glad to run into you, Boling. I have an idea we may do business." He dropped his hands carelessly into the pockets of a tailored black coat. "My firm is prepared to bid high for prime beef. Market's a little tight this year and a man has to cover all angles."

Carse said, "We've always dealt with Archer. They get first bid on Coffin beef."

Kellerway did not lose his smile. "I have a connection with your partner." Kellerway's eyes were brown, but of a different shade than his sister's. There was a lot of yellow in them. "You never can tell what might happen between now and shipping time."

Carse studied him. The man was handsome. A slight bulge at the left side of the coat told Carse that he carried a revolver.

"If Staggart goes east with the beef train this year," Kellerway said smoothly, "perhaps you and Mrs. Staggart would honor my sister and me at supper some evening."

"Mrs. Staggart goes nowhere without her husband."

"Oh, I understood you and Emily Staggart were—well, very close."

Carse said, "I don't like the insinuation," and raised a clenched fist.

Before Kellerway could reply, Allie flung herself between them. "I doubt if Mr. Staggart would find it amusing," she snapped at Carse, "if you and my brother fought over the reputation of Mrs. Staggart."

Carse looked down at her angry face. He revised his original impression of her. She wasn't pretty. There was too much bone in her face. And her mouth—well, it was an Irish mouth, he decided, and it should be smiling. But it wasn't smiling, and there were small half-moons at each corner.

Ignoring Kellerway, he said, "Tell your brother that the next time he mentions Mrs. Staggart's name in my presence he'll be lucky to be up and around in time to conduct his business at shipping time."

He turned from Allie to Paul Kellerway and their eyes held. He knew that here was a shrewd and dangerous opponent. And as he had done so many times in the past weeks, he felt that life was closing in on him.

"Do you ever carry a Sharps rifle?" he asked Kellerway.

Kellerway's thin dark brows lifted. "No," he said.

"I'll find out if you do," Carse said. "Or if you know someone who does."

He went out and Allie said, "Paul, what did he mean about a Sharps rifle?"

"Nothing," Paul Kellerway said, but Allie sensed that something Carse Boling had said had shaken her brother. She went to the store window and watched Carse cross the street on his long legs. Why had she acted like an idiot and made an issue over the women he had known? she asked herself. She had inadvertently overheard Si Gorman chiding him about it. She felt like a fool. And the remark she had caustically made about Mrs. Staggart . . . After all, she knew nothing about the woman; only what she had overheard Paul discussing with another man.

"Don't get interested in Carse Boling," Paul said, coming to stand at her side.

She laughed. "I'm hardly interested. I hope you noticed the way I talked to him."

"I noticed," he said. "Just stay away from him."

"I don't like you giving me orders, Paul."

Sensing he had angered her needlessly, Kellerway gave her his quick warm smile. "After all, you're my sister."

"Half sister," she corrected.

"I know what's best for you when it comes to men. Carse Boling isn't good for you."

Again she laughed, but this time her voice was shaky. "That's the most ridiculous assumption I've ever heard." She made a vague gesture, wondering why she was troubled. "Besides, he's going to be married. To Staggart's niece."

Kellerway rubbed his chin. "I didn't know that."

Allie said, "I don't see why you pick this late date to give me advice. You never bothered with any in all the years you were away from home. Only when Father died and you learned that I was left two thousand dollars and some land. Then you came home and wanted to borrow the two thousand for your grand venture."

He glanced nervously across the store at Si Gorman. "Believe me, Allie, you should go home," Kellerway said seriously. "I've tried to tell you all along that this is no business for a girl."

"You might call it protecting my investment," she said, trying to make her voice light. "I want to see that my two thousand dollars isn't spent unwisely."

"I'll take care of it, and take care of you. Only go home and wait until I can send you a share of the profits."

She was watching Carse Boling through the window, seeing that he was on the opposite side of the street now, talking to Sheriff Alcorte in front of the saddle shop. Her heart began that crazy lurching again, but she was certain it was the loathing she felt for a man who would steal his partner's wife.

"Perhaps I'll take your advice, Paul," she said. "I'll think about it."

In front of the saddle shop Carse had a few words with Sheriff Luke Alcorte. The Sheriff was a lank, mustached man whose thin face made one aware of the constant troubles of his office. He had a large nose, which he blew whenever he became nervous. Now he removed the bandanna from his hip pocket and gave a generous blow, for Carse had just told him about the shooting of Hank Peavey.

"And you figure the bullet was aimed at you?" the Sheriff said. When Carse nodded, Alcorte said, "But who'd want to shoot you?"

"There's some possibilities," he said grimly.

The Sheriff seemed to read some hidden meaning into his words, for he bristled. "Now see here, Carse. Don't you go thinkin' the Radich boys had anything to do with it."

"I didn't mention their names. You did." The Radich brothers had always campaigned strongly for Alcorte at election time. They expected favors and got them.

Alcorte flushed. "Every time there's trouble around here, folks pick on Bert and Ardo. Now, where did you say the shooting took place?" When Carse told him the details, the Sheriff gave another vigorous blast into the bandanna and stowed it in his hip pocket. "I'll have a look, Carse." Abruptly he changed the subject. "I figure we'll have a minimum of trouble this year at shipping time. I'm going to enforce the no-gun rule in town. You tell your boys."

"A good idea," Carse agreed, and wondered if Alcorte could make it stick.

Sheriff Alcorte said, "Sam Jedrow's in town. He's spread the word that he's been made *segundo* at Coffin."

"That boy's going to hang himself yet," Carse said.

When Carse started along the walk, the Sheriff said, embarrassed, "I just want you to know, Carse, that I don't believe a damn word about"—he blew his nose vigorously —"about you and Emily. It's Staggart's place to hush up talk like that. I'm surprised he ain't done it before this."

The cords tightened in Carse's neck. He went on down the street to Oren Goodfellow's saloon.

There were only half a dozen men at the bar. The interior was dim and cool and a relief from the heat that lay over Chicago Street. The air smelled faintly of damp sawdust. Carse knew most of the men; they greeted him with a certain reserve and he knew it was because of the ugly rumors that had been spread about him.

Oren Goodfellow picked a glass off the backbar with a long-fingered hand, blew dust from it, and placed it on the bar in front of Carse. Then he got a bottle.

"Heard about Sam Jedrow being named *segundo* at Coffin," Goodfellow said. "I always figured if a *segundo* was named, it would be Mrs. Staggart's brother, Johnny."

Carse poured a drink and took it fast. The whisky jolted him.

"Jedrow asks too many questions," Goodfellow said. "Stag has a lot of friends in this country. Si Gorman and me and Big Min, to name a few."

"Jedrow's been asking questions of them?"

"Yeah." Goodfellow had thinning yellow hair, which he

parted far down on the right side and plastered across his balding dome. Several times a day he would turn as he did now, study the reflection of his long face in the back-bar mirror, dip a hand in the tank, and brush wet finger-tips over his head to keep the hair in place.

He wore a flowered vest and a thick watch chain across his narrow middle. "I was in here the day Jedrow come in on the train," Goodfellow said, turning back to Carse. "Stag was playing poker, and when he saw Jedrow he dropped his cards on the floor. I think Stag aged ten years in that first minute he saw Jedrow."

In the distance sounded the faint blast of a train whistle. Men scrambled for the door. The arrival of the weekly train to Bellfontaine was an event. Carse took a deep breath, remembering why he had come to town this day.

He paid for his drink and stepped to the veranda. As he went down the steps he saw a rider just dismounting from a dun horse at the rack. It was Art Quince, a red-haired man with a laughing, freckled face. Art Quince fancied himself a gambler, and when his money would run out, Carse always had a job for him at Coffin.

Quince did not smile this day when he saw Carse. He seemed embarrassed.

Carse said, "I thought it was about time you showed up, Art. We're hiring again for roundup."

Quince ran the palms of his hands along his black pants. Though he was only in his middle twenties, his face already showed the lines of a heavy drinker. He wore a revolver, and from the patches on his clothing Carse knew Art Quince's luck this summer had not been good. They shook hands and for a moment Quince's tight gray eyes softened.

"Where you been all summer?" Carse asked.

Art Quince's old grin flickered a moment. "You can't beat roulette. You sure can't beat it."

"I tried to tell you that last year. There's a job for you at Coffin if you want it."

"I already got me a job, Carse," Quince said, and blushed. "A fella's got to make a dollar where he can."

Thoughtfully Carse studied his friend's face. Quince needed a shave and his gaze was not steady. Carse said, "You remember Hank Peavey, who helped Ben Smiley at the cook shack? Well, he got killed today."

"The hell you say!"

"Yeah. I don't figure Sheriff Alcorte will do anything about it. But I will. You understand that, Art?"

Quince's gray eyes darted everywhere but at Carse's face. "Hell, you don't figure I had anything to do with it, do you?"

"Just let me know if you see anybody who carries a Sharps rifle."

"Sure. Sure, I'll do that, Carse. I'll sure do that."

"Luck on the new job, Art," Carse said.

A thin man with a spike beard came out of the alley beside Goodfellow's. He wore greasy denims and his boots were cracked. He had hard eyes in a hard face. He came up to Quince and the latter introduced him to Carse as Ed Lopart.

At that moment Carse saw Sam Jedrow and Paul Kellerway come to the veranda of the Empire Hotel across the street. The two men stood talking together.

Lopart nudged Quince. "Kellerway wants us."

Lopart started across the street and Quince looked at Carse, his face red. "You understand how it is, Carse. A man's got to make a dollar where he can."

Carse said, "I understand now, Art. You're working for them." He looked beyond Quince to Jedrow and Kellerway on the hotel porch. "If this thing comes to a showdown, Art," Carse said, "I'd hate to be looking at you on the wrong side of the fence."

When Quince had gone to join Kellerway and Jedrow and Lopart, Carse thought: So that's how it is. Whatever it is Jedrow is up to, he isn't doing it alone.

Thoughtfully he walked to the railroad station just in time to be sprayed with steam from the engine. A girl was the only passenger. Pale and slender, she wore a gray cloak.

Carse went to her and removed his hat. "Miss Lenrick?"

"You must be Carse Boling. Uncle Martin wrote that you would probably meet me."

Carse felt a slight irritation at Stag's assumption that he would meet the train. She took his arm and he maneuvered her through the crowd of rough men who watched her. She seemed shy and a little faint from the heat. As they walked uptown she watched him from the corners of her gray eyes. He felt her studying him, and he thought then that he could at least have done her the courtesy of wearing his suit instead of work clothes.

"I'm glad Uncle Martin couldn't come," she said, and smiled. He found the smile interesting. There seemed to be a lack of warmth; it was a simple spreading of the red lips across the teeth.

"One thing you've got to remember, Miss Lenrick," he said. "Your uncle doesn't like to be called Martin."

"Oh, yes. I remember Mamma saying one time that Uncle Martin—I mean Stag—was very particular about his name. Odd, isn't it?"

As they moved up the street to Si Gorman's, where he had left the wagon, Margretha asked him questions about the country. And was it possible for a girl to find a store in town that would keep her well dressed?

"You talk like you plan to stay a while, Miss Lenrick."

They were crossing the street and she took his arm. He could feel the tips of her fingers exploring his biceps.

"There are lots of things I like already about this place," Margretha said.

Sam Jedrow crossed over and blocked them on the walk. He looked big and tough in his black suit. He took off his flat-crowned hat. His hair grew to a low V on his forehead. "I see you've met the girl," he said to Carse, and eyed Margretha. "Sure is a looker. Don't blame Stag for wanting you to marry her."

Carse heard Margretha giggle. "Marriage? Why, I had no idea." She peered up at Carse, and smiled at him.

"Glad to see you like the idea, miss," Jedrow said, hunching his immense shoulders. "It'll make things easier."

"That's enough, Jedrow," Carse said, not wishing Stag's niece to witness the ugly scene that must inevitably follow if this line of talk continued.

He moved with Margretha to the loaded wagon in front of Gorman's. Passers-by were looking at him and at Jedrow. Some of Goodfellow's customers had come to the porch of the saloon across the street. Carse lifted Margretha onto the wagon seat.

Jedrow came up and said, "Miss Lenrick, you and Carse getting married real quick will sure help keep down the gossip."

Carse had his back to Jedrow, and he jerked free the Winchester from the scabbard lashed to the wagon.

Jedrow said, "I'm not wearing a gun. But there's another way to settle this." He balled his big hands into fists.

Margretha screamed as Carse faced around in time to see Jedrow lunge at him. Carse reversed the rifle, extending the butt as if it were a bayonet.

The rifle butt caught Jedrow hard in the stomach. The big man went to his knees and rolled off the walk, gasping for breath. Men had come running up.

Dave Shell, the fat, curly-haired barber, cried, "You better get out of here, Carse. If he ever uses them spurs on you—"

"He won't," Carse said. He looked down at Jedrow's face, which seemed to have turned green. "Jedrow, if you've got any sense you'll clear out of this country." Then he levered in a shell as Ed Lopart and Art Quince came loping up from the hotel. Carse said, "You boys buying into this?"

Ed Lopart looked at Jedrow on the ground. "You're pretty tough, Boling," he said.

Carse turned to Quince. "Art, if you play with these rattlesnakes you're going to get hurt. There's still a job at Coffin if you want it."

Quince looked shamefaced, but he helped Lopart get the shaking Jedrow on his feet.

Carse drove to the station and got Margretha's portmanteau; then he headed for the ferry.

Margretha tied a scarf over her pale hair to keep off the dust. "So Uncle Stag wants us to marry. I might like that. Who knows?"

Her laughter made him feel uncomfortable, and somehow he was reminded of Della, the girl he had known so long ago back in Texas.

He said coolly, "This marriage business is Stag's idea, not mine."

"You mean you wouldn't want me?" She seemed surprised.

The sun was hot on his back as they angled down the slant to the river; he felt irritable. He thought of the kid who had died this day, of Sheriff Alcorte's lack of interest in the matter. Only with Min and the Sheriff had he discussed the passing of Hank Peavey. But he knew that within the hour the story would be all over town. He knew the first thing he would do when he got home. He would go into the kitchen and take Staggart's Sharps rifle down from its pegs and sniff the barrel to see if it had recently been fired.

Chapter Six

MARGRETHA CLUNG to Carse's arm as the wagon jolted across the logs of the landing. "What hateful country!" she said, as the ferry carried them toward the west bank. She stared at the flats, shimmering now in the September heat. "Whatever a person gained in this country would be earned. Earned the hard way."

"It's no country for a woman," Carse said.

"It would be if she shared it with a man." They were passing through a thick growth of willows. "Uncle Stag wrote me all about you. You own twenty per cent of Coffin. And if we marry he'll give you a full interest."

Carse pulled up the team beneath a towering bank; to their left the Missouri rolled southward. "So you and your uncle have planned this thing," he snapped.

His voice was harsh and she looked frightened and dug her fingers into the sleeves of his shirt. "Don't be angry," she whispered. She looked at him out of her long gray eyes, then put her forehead against his arm. "Don't be angry." They sat that way a moment on the wagon seat, then she turned and pointed at a spot where greenery was heavy at the riverbank. "It was such a hot and dusty ride on the train. I'd like to wash. Will you wait?"

Before he could reply, she had stepped down and was running toward the river. She removed the scarf and her long pale hair floated behind her. Then the willows hid her. In a few moments he saw her in the river, saw her bare white arms and shoulders. He swung down and rolled a cigarette. He felt tense. Then he saw the ugly mark on the wagon where the spent bullet from the Sharps had struck the wood. Whatever desire he might have felt was gone.

He called to her, "Hurry up. It'll be dark before we reach Coffin."

Either she didn't hear him or she chose to ignore his order. In a moment she screamed, and he ran into the willows and leaped over the neat pile she had made of her clothing. He saw her near the bank, only her head out of the water, her wet hair plastered to her shapely skull.

"Carse, I think I'm in quicksand."

"Hang on," he told her, and kicked off his boots.

He waded out into the river and felt the current tug at him. He reached her and, embarrassedly, put his arms about her. He was able to pick her up easily; he felt no pull of quicksand. He carried her up the bank and set her down, and saw an odd little smile on her lips.

And he knew.

"Damn you," he said. "The Missouri River is no place to play a joke."

She laughed. "But you came for me. You couldn't help yourself."

"Get dressed," he said gruffly, and stomped back to the wagon.

In a few minutes she joined him. As they drove toward Coffin she dried her hair on the scarf. "One thing I'll say about you, Mr. Boling," she told him thinly. "You're a man of exceptional will power."

He didn't bother to answer her. At the junction of the Coffin road and the one leading to Forty-four he saw the Radich brothers, Bert and Ardo. The men removed their hats when Carse pulled up and introduced Margretha.

"They run the biggest ranch in these parts," Carse explained to the girl.

Bert Radich was stocky, thick through the neck and shoulders. He had a fine curly black beard, in which he took great pride. "Didn't know Stag had a looker like you for kinfolk," Bert said.

Ardo Radich said, "Bert's right. Bert sure is right." He was half the size of his older brother. A small, dainty man, Ardo lived in Bert's shadow.

They talked about the roundup next week and the beef market. Then Carse said, "I hear you boys are itching to expand again."

"Well, a fella's got to grow," Bert Radich said, and combed fingers through his luxuriant beard. He was fifty, but there was no gray in his hair. "You and Stag gettin' worried we might push over your way?"

"Not at all, Bert." He looked Bert Radich in the eye. "That's one thing that don't worry us."

Bert sat his saddle, smiling a little. "I tell you one thing, Carse. As long as you're roddin' Coffin, we'll think twice about movin' your way."

"You do that, Bert." He paused, then said, "By the

way, I hear you don't like it much that Paul Kellerway is trying to line up Ralph Shamley and some of the other small outfits."

"It ain't that I don't like it, but I figure we ought to see what Kellerway is up to. So far as I know, nobody ever heard of that packing house he's supposed to rep for."

"Well, there's trouble kicking up for sure, Bert," Carse said. "I just want you and me to be in the open in this thing."

"How you mean, Carse?"

"Somebody tried to kill me this morning. They got Hank Peavey instead." He heard Margretha's quick indrawn breath at his side.

Bert Radich swore softly. "I'd watch myself from here on out, Carse. And watch that bronc buster you got over there. Sam Jedrow. I hear Stag has given him the run of the place. I don't like him worth a damn."

"Jedrow's been made *segundo*."

"Stag sure as hell has lost his mind now," Bert Radich said.

"Bert's right," Ardo said. "Bert sure is right."

They parted then and Carse continued on toward Coffin. When they were some hundred yards from the junction, Margretha said, "So a man was killed this morning. It must have been a great shock. No wonder you didn't want to—" She broke off and flushed.

"Didn't want to what?"

"Nothing."

The meeting between Stag and his niece was strained. They had buried Hank Peavey that afternoon, because there was no sense in postponing it. Peavey had no relatives in Dakota and there would be no preacher in Bellfontaine until shipping season. Stag seemed morose and Emily said it was a shame that a boy so young had to die. Carse had not told Emily or Stag that Hank Peavey's death was unintentional; that he had been the real target.

During the day his things had been moved into the lean-to at the end of the bunkhouse. Ben Smiley came by, saddened. He blamed himself for telling Hank Peavey he could go to town. When Smiley had gone, Carse went through Peavey's belongings and found the address of a married sister in Colorado. He wrote a letter to the woman, made a bundle of her brother's effects, then enclosed

Peavey's salary. He put in an extra fifty dollars of his own. Then he gave the bundle to one of the men to take to town.

Restlessly he paced the small room, thinking how Emily had looked when they had arrived from town. She wore a white dress and high heels. He could not help appreciating how mature she looked; not at all like the backwoods girl who had cooked his breakfast for so long. He was going to miss those mornings. Somehow seeing Emily's warm smile started the day right.

He fell to thinking of Margretha, half regretting that he had been a stiff-necked fool today at the river. But damn it, he thought, a man likes to make his own situations.

Johnny D'Orr came in and put an elbow against the roll-top desk. "Jedrow come in just now," he said. "He's makin' talk against you. Claimed you jumped him in town."

Carse told him about the brief fight.

Johnny's dark face was tight. "The fight was over you and Emily?"

Carse beat a fist into the palm of his hand. "I hate to kill a man. But it looks as if there's going to be no choice."

Johnny said, "When the moon is down, you better stay home of a night. Jedrow's the kind to wait for the long shadows to 'bush a man. Wouldn't surprise me none if Jedrow hasn't got Indian blood in him." Johnny's voice was bitter. "It's a dirty redskin trick to 'bush a man."

"Quit it," Carse said, and slapped the younger man lightly on the arm. "I probably have some Injun in me too. My grandpa was running around the Comanche country before he joined up with Taylor and went to Mexico."

Johnny D'Orr laughed without pleasure. "Thanks, you old Comanche. But nobody in this country saw you carried on your mother's back. They saw me."

"And they saw Emily," Carse cut in. It irritated him whenever Johnny felt sorry for himself. "Emily has put all that behind her. Why can't you? She's proud of being half Oglala. She doesn't give a damn who knows it."

"Emily's got what they call character."

"And so have you." Carse got up from his cot. He put a hand on Johnny's shoulder. "You're whiter than most men in this country."

"Next time we ride to Bellfontaine, explain that to Oren

Goodfellow. Explain to him how I'm whiter than most men and how it's all right for him to sell me whisky."

Carse changed the subject and talked about Margretha, but Johnny was paying little attention. Then he said, a sudden urge to escape the pressure coming over him, "You stick close to me, Johnny. Maybe when roundup's over we'll take a ride down to Texas. I'll show you some real country. Maybe we'll stay there and I'll have Stag send me money for my interest in the ranch."

"Thanks, Carse, but I'm staying here. I'm seeing that Stag plays fair with Emily and doesn't try to kick her out because she's a half-breed."

"That was a hell of a thing to say. Stag's in love with Emily. He's treated her fine." He thought of Stag's annual pilgrimage to Big Min's and his gaze avoided Johnny's.

Johnny said, "Stag has changed. I wonder how different things would be if Emily was your wife."

The door opened and Staggart appeared with a quart of whisky. His pale eyes touched Johnny D'Orr, and Carse wondered if the rancher had overheard the talk about Emily.

Carse forced a grin. "Nice of you to bring a drink, Stag. Welcome to my new quarters."

Staggart sat down on the cot. "Well, how do you like Margretha?" And when Carse said she was a good-looking girl, Stag shoved the bottle at him. "Drink to her." His voice was thick and Carse knew this wasn't the only bottle Stag had had this day.

Carse took a drink, to be polite, and passed the bottle to Johnny, although he knew Emily's brother would not touch it. Johnny stepped to the door. "Whisky in the same room with an Indian is bad medicine." He gave Staggart a hard look. "The fumes might set me off, even if I don't drink. And I'd sharpen my knife and go looking for scalps." He went out, slamming the door.

"What the hell's ailing him?" Stag wanted to know. When Carse made no reply, the rancher said, "I hear you and Jedrow went at it in town."

"Yeah."

"I want you to stay away from him."

Carse said, "Either he's stirring up the talk about Emily and me or he knows who is." He told Stag about Paul Kellerway and Jedrow with their heads together in town today. "I don't know what connection there is between you and Jedrow. But if you don't care if Emily's good name is dragged in the mud, I do. The next time Jedrow opens his mouth about her I'll shut it for him."

He opened a desk drawer and removed a belted gun rig. This he slung around his middle.

Staggart turned away and Carse felt sickened when he saw the man's face sag, saw the fear in his eyes. Staggart had been a tough and ruthless baron of the saddle and he had shrewdly built one of the largest ranches in the territory. Yet in a matter of weeks Carse had witnessed a slow disintegration in the man.

There was pleading in Staggart's eyes. "Let it ride."

"You can't ignore the talk about Emily."

Staggart took another drink. "Just wait till after roundup. That's all I ask." He beat a clenched fist on the top of the iron safe at the end of Carse's bunk.

"And I'm also supposed to stand by and let you make him *segundo* when you know you promised the job to Johnny."

Some of the old belligerence crept into Staggart's voice. "You figure your twenty per cent gives you the right to tell me who to hire?"

"That's the way I figure, Stag," Carse said quietly. From the bunkhouse next door came the sounds of men talking. There was not the customary noise, the high good humor. This day one of their number had died. It had cast a pall over the ranch.

Staggart tried to quell his fear with bluster. Then, failing, he said, "Sam Jedrow's an old friend. I owe him some money. He'll be gone after roundup."

"I wish I could believe he'll be gone."

Staggart snapped, "You keep at a man, Carse. I ask you to do one simple thing and you keep at me. I want you to keep clear of Jedrow. I'm asking you this one thing."

"It's a lot to ask." Carse watched Staggart move angrily to the door and said, "You haven't said one word about Hank Peavey's getting killed."

Stag turned. "It was an accident, wasn't it? Likely somebody drawing a bead on a deer and didn't know you and Peavey was anywheres near."

Carse said, "It was a bullet from a Sharps rifle that killed him."

Staggart glowered from under bushy brows. "I got a Sharps, but I sure as hell didn't shoot that kid. I'd have no reason."

"But you might have a reason to shoot me. Because of Emily."

Staggart's mouth opened. "That rifle ain't been fired in six months."

"I hope so, Stag. I sure hope so."

Staggart began to bluster again. "What was you and Johnny talkin' about when I come in here?"

Carse said, "Johnny sometimes can't get over the fact that his grandpa was an Oglala chief. That's what we were talking about."

Staggart licked the underside of his mustache. "I thought I heard him say something about Emily and you."

"You're mistaken," Carse lied, and in a moment Staggart took his bottle and went back to the house.

Carse waited for some minutes, then went out into the darkness. He crossed to the house and entered by the kitchen door. He lifted his long arms and took down the Sharps rifle from its pegs. It had not been fired; there was no odor of powder at the muzzle. He replaced the gun and then looked around to see Emily in the doorway.

She seemed to read his mind. "Stag didn't leave the ranch today. He couldn't have killed the Peavey boy."

She crossed to him, peering up at his face out of troubled dark eyes. "Somebody meant to kill you. And Hank Peavey died by mistake."

He put his hands on her shoulders, feeling the small bones under his fingers. "Emily, you've got enough to worry about. Stag asked me to let things ride till after roundup. I'm going to do my best to leave it that way. Because if I don't, this whole ranch can be wrecked. Let's get the herd ready for shipment. Then we'll see what this business means."

"A boy was killed today. Doesn't anyone intend to do anything about it?"

"I do, Em. Give me time. Just give me time."

Margretha came to the door and Carse removed his hands from Emily's shoulders. "I'm sorry," Margretha said. "I should have knocked. I'll remember whenever you two are alone together."

Carse stiffly told Emily good night. He did not look at Margretha.

Chapter Seven

THE ROUNDUP occupied all of Carse Boling's time during the next two weeks. It was hot, grueling work. He noticed that the enthusiasm of former years was lacking. It seemed the entire crew had sensed the widening chasm between the two partners. Since the day he had brought her to Coffin, Carse had not seen Margretha Lenrick.

At roundup Staggart seemed more morose than usual and Carse knew the man was burdened with some desperate problem. That Jedrow and perhaps Kellerway were blackmailing Staggart, Carse had no doubt. Stag neglected his job and at night he would ride to headquarters to see Emily. But after the first week he did not go to the ranch.

One thing Carse had insisted on. He would not have Jedrow at the roundup camp. Jedrow was staying at the home ranch.

After his last trip to headquarters Staggart was worse. He drank at night and during the day. Carse would find the rancher watching him. It began to get on Carse's nerves. He sensed that Staggart and Emily had had a fight the last time Stag had gone home.

One morning, when the gather had grown to fifteen hundred head, Carse said, "Why don't you and Em make it up?"

Staggart was at the chuck wagon drinking his morning coffee. "We been fighting over you," he said savagely. "She's in love with you."

"That's a damn lie and you know it."

Carse turned away, feeling a sense of guilt. For he remembered what Johnny had said: "Emily's been in love with you for years." He watched the dust kicked up by cow hands working the herd. "This sounds like more of Jedrow's talk," he said at last.

Staggart made no reply to that. Lines had deepened on his face and there were pouches under his eyes. Ben Smiley and his crew were cleaning up after breakfast. There was the bawling of angry steers. Riders pounded into camp, changed horses, then rode out again. The small outfits,

Shamley's Anchor, Tucker's LX, and Carter's Spade, were on the left side of the camp. The Radich brothers occupied the whole end of the valley across from Coffin.

Staggart said, "You ain't been making much headway with my niece."

"How can I court a girl and work roundup?" Carse demanded.

Staggart scratched a thumbnail through his bristle of whiskers. "Seems like you always had plenty of time for them other women. The redheaded widow and—"

"Stag, I've had about enough of this!"

Staggart hurled his coffee cup into the dishpan under the tailboard of the chuck wagon. When he stalked off, Ben Smiley wiped his hands on his flour-sack apron. "Stag has sure 'nough got a burr up his butt," the old cook observed.

"If he's got one," Carse said, "it's of his own doing."

Emily was alone that day at headquarters. Margretha had gone for a ride and the crew was doing the chores. She had just finished cleaning up the kitchen when she saw Sam Jedrow in the doorway. The sight of the big man made her weak in the knees, and she wanted to cry out for help. But there was no one to hear her.

She said, "Get out of here, Jedrow."

He moved deeper into the kitchen, the chime of those awful spurs sounding like a dirge to her on this quiet, sunny morning. "Mrs. Staggart, I—" He put out his big hands toward her.

She recoiled and snatched up a butcher knife and held it in front of her. "I'll kill you if you touch me."

"I'd like to talk. Only talk."

She turned to flee and he leaped for her and caught her around the waist and took the knife from her hand. He flung it across the room. Then he turned her loose and she fled down the hallway.

"I want to tell you about Lydia!" he shouted, and followed her into the bedroom.

She had taken a revolver from a bureau drawer and now she leveled it at him. "Get to the roundup camp, Jedrow. I won't say what happened here today. If I did, my husband would kill you."

"You mean Carse Boling would—or try to. Your husband ain't got the guts, Mrs. Staggart." His wide scarred face was dark with angry blood. "And to hell with you. If you think I come in this house to—to— Well, I come to talk, nothing else."

When he had gone, Emily sank wearily to the bed. In a moment she heard him ride out.

Carse saw Jedrow at camp when he came in with the day's gather. They had been out in the jack-pined hills. Johnny D'Orr had narrowly missed getting gored by a cow. Already in a foul mood because of the heat and the dust and the monotony, Carse exploded when he saw Jedrow.

He called Staggart aside. "I told you I wouldn't work roundup with him."

Staggart nearly had tears in his eyes. "Bear with me, Carse. That's all I ask. Bear with me."

"Why'd he come out here to camp?"

"I don't know. But let him stay. Let him stay." Staggart looked old and sick.

"Stag, I'm going to tell you something. I've just about had a bellyful of this. You tell me why Jedrow's in Dakota and why you're afraid to move against him. Either that or I'm riding out. I'll cut my twenty per cent of the herd and go."

Staggart's face seemed to break apart. "Stay till after we ship. Then if you want to pull out, we'll get a lawyer and do it right."

Carse's mouth was dry. He had been this man's partner for seven years. And now it was to end like this. Just get a lawyer and do it right. He was about to say, "The hell with you," when he noticed, as he had so many times in recent weeks, the lurking fear in the depths of Staggart's pale eyes. Despite the man's obvious cowardice, he could not help feeling a measure of pity.

Unable to sleep that night, Carse left his blankets and rode the sixteen miles to headquarters, arriving shortly after sunup.

While the crew was on roundup Emily did the cooking for the few hands left at headquarters. Carse found her in the kitchen, frying beans and beef. Her quick smile warmed him. He took her hands. "Did something happen here? Between you and Jedrow?"

There was nothing to read in her Indian face. "Nothing happened, Carse. Why do you ask?" Then she said, "Does

your coming here mean you and Stag have had trouble?"
Her voice was worried and he knew that she was concerned about the stupidly jealous man who was her husband.

She sank to a bench and Carse said, "He doesn't deserve a woman like you, Emily." He helped himself to a
cup of coffee. "Stag's acting like a crazy man. One reason
I came was to see if he's given you any hint of why he's
afraid of Jedrow."

Emily shook her dark head. "He knew Jedrow somewhere before. For some reason the man has a hold on him.
But I don't know why."

Grimly Carse sipped his coffee. "There's still that talk
about you and me."

She laughed bitterly. "Stag wouldn't face it. He thought
it would end if he got you to marry his niece." Emily
looked at him. "You're not really going to marry her, are
you?"

He rubbed the back of his neck. "Of course, there's the
fifty per cent of Coffin Stag offered me if I put a ring on
her finger."

Emily rose from the bench and walked to the window
and gazed out upon the yard, where the headquarters crew
was just emerging from the bunkhouse. They were stretching and scratching themselves as they lined up at the
washstand and pumped the tank full of water. Those that
still had hair combed it. Most of the men left behind were
too old or crippled up to be of much use at roundup.

Emily said, "Stag is afraid. A long time ago he did
something he's ashamed of. And now it's come home to
face him."

"There's hardly a man in this country that doesn't have
something to hide. This is rough country and it was built
by rough men."

Emily turned wearily to the stove as the men started
moving toward the kitchen. "You'd best get back to camp
before Stag finds you came here."

He went to her and put his hands at her small waist
and she leaned back against him. In that moment he felt
very warm and solid and good, as if his troubles had all
been solved by the simple act of touching this woman. He
had lived with her under this roof for three years; he had
heard her sing as she cooked breakfast. It was the first
time they had ever stood together this way.

"You're too fine a woman to put up with what you have here at Coffin," he told her.

She turned then, looking up into his face. "Stag is my husband. You're his partner. Please try to get along with him. For my sake. I'm hoping this delusion of his will pass."

He saw that she had been very pale, but now the color was back in her pretty face. She began to cook the men's breakfast with her old efficiency, and he realized that she had put a barrier between them. In a way, he was glad. She would have too much conscience ever to go behind Stag's back and enjoy the going.

Carse went to the yard, passed the time of day with the men converging on the kitchen, and then went on to the big empty bunkhouse. He went to Jedrow's bunk and drew out the cowhide trunk Jedrow had opened the other day. It was locked. He turned the trunk over and with the blade of his knife cut a slit in the back. He found clothing and some cartridges. He found a derringer with a special holster that had a spring clip and thin leather straps. He judged it to be the type strapped to the arm and worn under a coat sleeve. The sort of weapon a card sharp might carry. Hardly a gun for a man who signed himself on at a ranch as bronc buster.

Carse found a photograph showing a much younger Sam Jedrow. With him was a man Carse recognized as Paul Kellerway. White ink at the bottom of the photo said it had been taken at the Acme Studios in Tucson.

He found a bill of sale for a chestnut horse. Then he came across a news clipping date-lined Mogollon, New Mexico. It concerned a man named Jim Martin, sentenced to hang in '72, who had escaped from jail the morning he was to be executed. The clipping was old and soiled and most of it had been torn off.

A sound caused him to turn, and he saw Margretha watching him from the doorway. It galled him that she had witnessed this sneaky business. "I'd appreciate it if you said nothing about this," he told her.

Her shoulders shrugged under a green dress. She wore long white gloves. "It's no concern of mine," she said, and her gray eyes watched him.

He returned Jedrow's belongings to the trunk and kicked it under the bunk.

"We don't seem to be making much progress," Margretha said. She rested the tip of a parasol between the narrow toes of her shoes. "Uncle Martin—I mean Stag—seems so intent on having us marry. I've hardly seen you. Does roundup keep you this busy?"

"It's not an easy job."

"When will I see you? I mean when will you take me to town for some fun?"

He told her there was yet much work to do. The cattle they intended to ship would have to be driven to Bellfontaine.

"Maybe you and I could ride the beef train to Chicago," Margretha said excitedly.

"Where'd you learn about the beef train?"

Her gray eyes were guarded. "I've picked up the talk from the men here."

He suddenly made up his mind to take the beef train to Chicago himself. "If you're still here when I get back from Chicago we'll talk about having fun."

Her face altered and there was a hardness about her mouth. "I'll still be here, never fear."

"There's nothing at Coffin to hold you," he said crisply.

"Perhaps you don't realize it, but I'm Stag's only heir. And if something happens to him—"

"You won't inherit Coffin, if that's what you're thinking." He had an urge to slap her across the face. "Stag's share of Coffin will go to Emily."

"I doubt if she's his legal wife. When a man takes a squaw into his blankets he rarely bothers to marry her."

Carse got her by an arm and flung her across the bunk. She lay there, glaring at him, for the moment not bothering to cover herself. At last she sat up and smoothed her dress.

"That was a pretty vile thing you said about Emily," Carse snapped.

"It might be the truth." Margretha got to her feet, her gray eyes angry. "And don't give me that smug look. After all, you're hardly lily white. You're a thief. Or can you explain what you were doing in Sam Jedrow's trunk?"

"How can you explain you knew it was Jedrow's trunk?"

She reddened and seemed confused.

He said, reading guilt in her eyes, "How was it with Jedrow? You and him alone here at the ranch. Did you use quicksand again for an excuse, as you did with me?"

He gave her a hard smile and brushed past her and

crossed to the house. The men had finished eating and were roping out their horses. He entered the kitchen.

Carse sat down beside Emily on a bench. Her head rested on her folded arms on the table. Slowly she raised her head and looked at him. He could tell she had been crying.

"I came here for one reason," he told her. "I wanted to go through Jedrow's trunk. And I did."

"You found something?"

He started to tell her, then knew it would only add to her worries. "Not a thing. But the trip won't be entirely wasted if I can cheer you up a little."

She sighed and leaned against him as if suddenly shorn of her strength. He lifted his arm and put it about her. She was small and slender and he could feel her warmth through the calico dress. He thought of what Johnny had said: "Emily's been in love with you for years." Somehow he felt guilty, as if in some unknown way this ugly talk about Emily were his fault. They sat together quietly while the headquarters crew rode out of the yard.

"I'm so tired, Carse," Emily said, and he sensed the strain she had been under, trying to keep Johnny from following a life of violence, trying to stem the rising jealousy of an older husband. Then she said in a sudden hoarse whisper, "Stag is at the door."

Carse felt a sudden tightening along the back of his neck. He looked over his shoulder and saw that Staggart had quietly opened the door leading to the yard. Stag stood in the opening, hunched over, his eyes bloodshot, his clothing filthy. A stubble of dirty beard darkened his cheeks. His mustache was ragged.

Stag had taken down his loaded Sharps rifle from the pegs above the kitchen door.

Chapter Eight

ONE GLANCE and Carse knew his partner was very drunk. He heard Emily give a little whimper and felt her stiffen at his side. There were fresh stains on the front of Stag's blue shirt, and they told Carse that the man had been drinking from a bottle as he rode from camp.

Stag shifted the Sharps a little. The lethal ball of screaming lead it could fire would smash into Carse and then into Emily. He thought of the wreckage such a bullet had done to Hank Peavey. He felt sick. He saw Stag's finger tighten on the trigger and a drop of sweat broke between his shoulder blades to run coldly down his back.

Slowly Carse got to his feet. "Stag, put up the rifle."

Staggart's lips parted below the ragged mustache. "Catched you cozy. Purely cozy."

"Wait a minute," Carse warned.

But Staggart shifted the muzzle of the rifle so that it was lined squarely on him. "I heard you sneaked back to Emily," Staggart said thickly. "But I didn't really believe it." He gestured with the rifle. "Set down there on the bench, boy. And get away from him, Em."

Emily finally found her voice. "Stay where you are, Carse," she said firmly.

From a corner of his eye Carse could see that she was white with fear. Stag lifted the rifle slightly so that Carse could stare into the deadly black maw of the big weapon. He realized it might very well be the last thing in this life he would ever see.

"You've let Jedrow poison your mind," Carse said.

Staggart only looked at him. A faint breeze stirred the kitchen curtains that yesterday Emily had starched and ironed. The breakfast dishes of the headquarters crew were stacked in a big pan.

"For God's sake, Stag," Carse said, "don't do something you'll be sorry for."

"I won't be sorry about killin' you," Staggart said. His face changed. "Some killin' I have been sorry for. But not this one." Staggart's mouth tightened. "Get clear of him, Em, or he'll splatter on you when I shoot him."

54

"You talk like a butcher," Emily said scornfully, trying to hide the fear in her voice.

Although he knew it would be a futile gesture, Carse was determined to knock Emily to the floor with one hand and try to get his gun at the same moment. Stag was grinning a little, his eyes hard and watchful, as if he were daring him to try.

At that moment there was movement at the door. Margretha Lenrick, wearing her long gloves, walked in from the yard. Pushing aside the barrel of the Sharps held by her uncle, she entered the kitchen. Her face was paler than usual, and a pulse throbbed wildly at her throat.

"Excuse me, Uncle Stag," she said, a ghastly smile on her lips. Then she addressed herself to Carse. "Did you find a sidesaddle?" she asked. "If not, I'll have to change. Perhaps Emily can lend me some of her riding clothes."

"They wouldn't fit," Emily said.

Margretha laughed shrilly. "If I'm going to marry Carse and live in this country, Uncle Stag, I might just as well learn to ride like a man." She turned then and faced Staggart, whose face had sagged. She lowered her gaze to the rifle. "Are you angry with me for taking Carse away from roundup?" she asked, as if perplexed by the formidable weapon he held.

Staggart sank to a bench and laid the Sharps on the table. "You took Carse away from camp?"

"Yes, I sent him a note last night by one of the riders. I thought Carse and I could have an early ride. Do you think it was foolish of me, Uncle Martin?"

Staggart stiffened on the bench. "How many times have I got to tell you not to call me Uncle Martin?"

Margretha went to him quickly and put her slender gloved hands on his shoulders and kissed his bristly cheek. "I'm sorry, Uncle Stag. But today I'm hardly myself." She stepped away from Stag and looked directly at Carse. "You see, this morning Carse asked me to be his wife."

Staggart let out a long sigh, and Carse, stony-faced, looked at Emily. For a second there was a stricken look in Emily's eyes, and then in their depths was a hard core of anger as she stared across the room at Margretha.

Margretha came to stand beside Carse. She took his arm in her two hands and hugged it to her. She beamed at her uncle. "I guess you didn't know, Uncle Stag, that Carse and I have been together many times."

Staggart ran a trembling hand over his dirty face. "Got some coffee, Em? We got to toast these two kids. And it's too early in the mornin' to be drinkin' whisky."

Emily filled four cups and set them on the table, murmuring, "It's never too early for you to drink whisky." But Stag did not hear her.

"By God, you kids sure had me fooled," Stag said. Then he gave Carse a sharp look. "The other day I mentioned that you and Margretha wasn't seeing much of each other. Why didn't you tell me then how things was between you?"

Margretha said quickly, "It was my fault. I wanted him to wait until we were sure." She stood on tiptoe and kissed Carse full on the mouth.

Laughing, Staggart slapped the table with the flat of his hand so hard that the big Sharps jumped under the impact.

Carse said, "You better unload that rifle before somebody gets killed around here."

Staggart gave him a hurt look. "I'm sorry, Carse. Damn if I ain't sorry."

Margretha seemed very gay. "We'll be married in town, Uncle Stag. The day you ship. Carse has promised me a party. Isn't that wonderful?"

Staggart grinned. "By hell, I can't get over how you had me fooled." Then he said with mock seriousness, "Carse, you better not shirk your job. We got a roundup to finish. Now you two kids go on outside. And if I catch you kissin' I'll look the other way." He rose from the bench and put a big hand on Carse's arm. "This makes me happy, Carse." The pale eyes were misty. "You'll be one of the family now." His voice rose, "And nothin' ever can touch Coffin. You hear that, Em?" He turned to his wife, who stood small and dark and troubled at the stove. "Nothin' can ever touch us, Em."

Staggart walked over and put his arm about Emily's waist. "A man gets damn lonesome at roundup. A man likes to ride in and see his wife. Now you kids clear out of here. A man likes to be alone with his wife."

Carse looked at Emily, who stood rigid beside Staggart. In a moment Staggart, chuckling, moved down the hall to the back part of the house. Emily turned and followed him.

In the yard with Margretha, Carse rolled a cigarette. His fingers were moist and trembling.

Margretha gave him an arch look. "He was going to kill you. Maybe kill both of you."

"I know."

"You'll have a fifty-per-cent interest in Coffin. Is that so bad?" When he remained silent, she looked at his face. It reminded her of hard brown rock. "The die is cast, as they say in books. You'll marry me now, Carse."

He caught her by the arms and swung her around so he could peer down into her startled face. "What do you want, Margretha? Not me. You're not in love with me. What is it?"

"I want half of Coffin," she told him bluntly.

Her gray eyes were wide and beautiful and she looked completely guileless. "It isn't easy for a girl living alone, Carse. I don't intend to go back to my former existence."

"I'm beginning to wonder just what sort of existence it was," he said coldly.

She looked at him, and there was that stirring of her lips meant for a smile. "You'll marry me, Carse. Remember that." She hurried into the house.

In a few minutes Staggart came out and they got their horses and rode slowly back to camp. On the way Staggart made his plans. They'd build a new house. Maybe Margretha and Carse would have kids. Stag would like that. Nothing like kids around the house. He was sorry that it looked as if he and Emily would never have any. With kids a man didn't mind working. Then he had something to leave his possessions to.

Carse said nothing, but he made up his mind that come shipping day he would be on the beef train bound for Chicago. Staggart could send him his interest in the ranch. If he refused that, Carse would put a lien against the cattle they shipped. He would get his 20 per cent, then go back to Texas.

When Carse and Staggart had ridden out of the yard, Margretha came into the kitchen and stripped off her gloves. She began to dry the dishes Emily washed.

Emily said, "This is surprising. It's the first time you've offered to help."

Margretha smiled in that secret way of hers. "You owe me your life. If I hadn't overheard Stag from the yard this morning, you and Carse would both probably be dead."

Emily paused, lifting her dripping hands from the dishpan. "I do appreciate what you did. It was a brave thing. Stag might have turned on you. A man crazy jealous like that—"

Margretha wiped a tin plate with a dish towel. "You're in love with Carse, aren't you?" And when Emily colored, Margretha went on: "Maybe Stag has a right to be jealous."

"There's nothing between Carse and me."

"But you wish there were."

Emily turned and looked up at the taller woman. "I think it was despicable the way you tricked Carse this morning. A man doesn't like a woman to trick him into marriage."

"Turnabout is fair play." Margretha laid the tin plate carefully on the table. "He already tricked *me*."

Emily's dark brows arched. "What does that mean?"

"Don't be naïve. You're a married woman."

Emily seemed startled, then said, "I don't believe you."

"I only tricked Carse this morning to protect myself," Margretha said. "I—I think I'm going to have a baby."

Emily searched the pretty pale face, then turned back to the dishpan. "You're lying," she said.

"Ask Carse if he had me naked on the bank of the Missouri River. Ask him that!" Margretha flung her dish towel onto the table and hurried from the room.

Chapter Nine

JUST BEFORE Carse and Staggart reached the roundup camp, Carse reined in his dun. "It was Jedrow that sent you after me this morning," Carse said.

Staggart colored. "I should have knowed there wasn't nothin' bad between you and Em."

Carse said, "Thanks for telling me. I just wanted to be sure."

He spurred his horse to the camp and straight across the holding grounds. Some of the cattle bellowed and a few horses in the *remuda* started kicking.

Bert Radich pushed his bearded face into the breeze and shouted, "Hey, Carse, you trying to set that herd to running? Slow down!"

Carse did not hear him. He wheeled into the herd where the riders were working their cutting horses. In the midst of the bawling cattle he found Sam Jedrow about to cut a big Coffin steer from the main herd. Carse rode up roughly and caught the man by a thick forearm and hauled him around, nearly spilling him from the saddle.

At the same moment Carse drew his gun and pressed the muzzle against the startled Jedrow's stomach. "You ever mention my name in the same breath with Emily Staggart's again, and I'll kill you."

Jedrow's green eyes looked down at the gun and then lifted to Carse's angry face. "The talk about you and Emily Staggart is the only thing I don't like about this deal. But the rest of it I like. And if you figure to pull that trigger, have at it. Because if you don't, one day I'm goin' to work your face over with my spurs. Work on it so no woman will ever look at you. Not even Emily Staggart."

Carse said, "Don't mention her name."

"Get that gun out of my guts," Jedrow said.

Carse holstered the weapon and wheeled away to the *remuda*. He was trembling when he got some coffee at the chuck wagon. Johnny D'Orr, his perspiring face smeared with dust, came trotting up.

"Damn it, Carse, if I was you I wouldn't put up with the lousy setup Stag is handing you."

Carse said, "It's what is known as protecting your investment."

Old Ben Smiley said, "Puttin' a gun on Jedrow ain't goin' to make him like you none."

For the next few days Carse Boling tried to throw himself wholeheartedly into the monotonous business of roundup. Those that had witnessed the incident between Carse and Jedrow made bets on when the thing would finally be settled.

Several times Staggart tried to discuss the matter with Carse. He became worried when Carse refused to talk about it. "But you and Margretha are still goin' to get hitched, ain't you?"

"So she says," Carse muttered.

One day Staggart found him at the chuck wagon just as the hands were finishing breakfast. Staggart had been sober since the incident at Coffin headquarters.

"I'm right sorry about the other day, Carse," Staggart said, shamefaced. "I—I was drunk and—"

"A Sharps rifle is a nasty weapon. It can knock a hole in a man big enough to put your boot through."

Staggart pleaded, "Don't be sore, Carse." He brightened. "Soon as you and Margretha are married, why don't you take a few months and show her St. Louis?"

"We'll talk about it later, Stag." Carse finished the inevitable beans and bacon on his plate. "Are we dealing with Archer as usual this year? Or have you got another packing house in mind?"

Staggart was wary. "Why'd you ask?"

"Just something Paul Kellerway said in town one day."

Staggart looked away. "Wherever we sell our beef, you'll get a full price for your share." Stag glanced at the sun. "I'm ridin' to town today. You take care of things here."

Carse said thinly, "Yeah, I guess you've got a lot of things to take care of in Bellfontaine. Paying Min in advance for your annual drunk, for one thing." Carse walked off.

As the roundup progressed, the camp moved to the eastern end of the range. This morning Carse rode out with Johnny D'Orr and some other Coffin hands to look for strays. They found twenty and drove them to the holding ground shortly before noon.

Johnny D'Orr said, "You watch out for Jedrow. He's got his eye on you."

Carse saddled up Jack, his cutting horse. He rode the horse into the morning's gather to cut out Coffin brands. Dust boiled up into the hot dome of the sky; it stung the nostrils and settled on the damp planes of his face. He got five Coffin steers shunted into the Coffin day herd. Then it was back into the dust again.

A big cow with the Coffin brand caught his eye. He shifted his body slightly in the saddle and Jack responded instinctively. The cutting horse edged toward the big animal. Carse could sense that Jack was wary, for already the big cow was short-tempered from being driven out of her favorite arroyo and held here in the blazing sun. Johnny D'Orr spurred up.

"A pecky cow," Carse called to Johnny D'Orr. "Stay away from her. She's a mean one. I'll take over."

The pecky cow was dangerous. Unlike a bull, which would charge blindly, a cow kept her eyes open. She tossed her horns and gave Jack and his rider a baleful look. From out of the dust a rope end suddenly appeared and caught the cow squarely between the horns. Carse swore under his breath and reined in Jack. Some dough-headed fool had misjudged the cow's position and struck it on the head instead of on the rump, antagonizing it.

Because he was only five yards or so from the cow, Carse tried to ride out of it. He looked to see who had struck the cow. Riding out of the dust was Sam Jedrow. The big man was standing up in the stirrups, a doubled rope end dragging on the ground.

Carse shouted, "Jedrow, stay back. I've got this one!"

Either Jedrow did not hear or he chose to ignore the order. He slapped at the cow with the rope, striking it across the eyes. With a snort of rage the cow tried to gore Jedrow's horse.

Expertly Jedrow maneuvered his mount away from the horns of the pivoting cow. The cow then turned on Carse, and he reined Jack quickly. As the cutting horse wheeled, its hind feet somehow got tangled up in Jedrow's dragging rope. Thrown off balance, Jack stumbled. The charging cow struck the horse squarely, and Carse was barely able to jerk free his right leg to save it from being shattered by the impact. As he fell he could hear the grating sound of horns against bone. Carse struck the ground hard, and rolled away as the cattle milled nervously. Through a break in the curtain of choking dust Carse saw his horse writhing on the ground. Rage leaped through him. Carse saw Jedrow fire a bullet into the head of the dying horse. Getting shakily to his feet, Carse reached for his gun, but the holster was empty. Before he could hunt for the weapon he was knocked off his feet by the rump of a lunging bull. Above the turmoil he heard Johnny D'Orr shouting his name.

"Carse!" Johnny yelled, and spurred through the frightened, bawling cattle and kicked a foot out of the stirrup. As he flashed by, Carse managed to grab stirrup and horn and hang on until they were clear of the herd. He had lost his hat and was bruised and jarred up. He swung down, trembling in his anger.

Miraculously the herd did not stampede. The riders circled warily.

Johnny asked anxiously, "You all right, Carse?"

Carse nodded and pushed the torn sleeve of a shirt across his forehead as Jedrow came up and dismounted. Jedrow stood tall and belligerent, thick through the chest and legs, a powerful man bent on destruction. For in the depths of the green eyes Carse could sense the man's determination to finish the thing that had been started this September day on the flats of Dakota Territory.

Jedrow said, "Sorry about your horse." Then he tramped over to the chuck wagon, where old Ben Smiley looked on worriedly. The other hands were tense, expectant.

Bert Radich came up, fluffing out his curling beard with the back of his hand. He saw Carse glaring at Jedrow.

"Only way to handle an *hombre* like that," Bert Radich observed, "is to use a gun. Don't try to fist-fight him, Carse. Otherwise me and Ardo might be tempted to make an offer for Coffin. 'Cause you wouldn't be around to keep pullin' Stag out of the hole."

"You praying for me or against me, Bert?" Carse said, his eyes still on Jedrow, who was pouring himself a cup of coffee.

"Coffin and Forty-four would make a sizable spread," Radich said.

His younger brother, Ardo, had come up. "Bert's right. Bert sure is right."

Carse walked toward the chuck wagon. An air of tension hung over the camp. It seemed that an unusual number of riders wanted coffee at this particular moment.

Even those that had been on night trick rose cautiously.

Carse said, "Get back on the job, boys." The inside of his mouth was dry. He saw Jedrow watching him across the cook fire, coffee cup held in a big hand.

Carse said after a minute, "Jedrow, you riled that cow deliberate."

Jedrow cuffed back his flat-crowned hat. He wore a yellow shirt. His striped pants were powdered with dust.

"A man better get himself a gun before he talks tough," Jedrow said.

"And after you got the cow mad enough," Carse plunged on, "you dropped your loop on the ground and Jack got tangled up in it."

"Ain't the first time a man dropped a rope accidental," Jedrow said.

"Did you figure I'd get pitched on my head and break my neck? Or at least have a steer horn through my skull before I could get off the ground?"

Jedrow said, "Hell, to hear you talk, a man would think I didn't like you."

Old Ben Smiley nervously wiped his hands on his apron. He picked up a short iron bar and started to lay it against the triangle, hoping to forestall trouble by calling the men to the noon meal.

"Hold it, Ben," Carse ordered. "We'll settle this thing. We can eat dinner later."

Jedrow said, "If you aim to push this thing, Boling, you better eat now. It'll be your last chance."

Carse jerked his thumb at the man. "You're fired. Get off Coffin!"

"I got money comin'!"

"I'll give you an I.O.U. Oren Goodfellow will cash it."

Jedrow's immense shoulders shrugged under his yellow shirt. He skirted the cook fire, as if to throw his tin cup into the dishpan under the tail gate of the chuck wagon. He had about a half cup of coffee left. This he hurled suddenly at Carse. Carse flung up his hands instinctively, but some of the hot coffee seared his right cheek. He did not take time to smear it away, but leaped at Jedrow and hit the man in the face. The solid smash of the fist sent Jedrow reeling against the chuck wagon. Closing in quickly, Carse belted him in the ribs.

The cry went up: "Carse Boling and Jedrow are goin' at it!" Men came running.

Chapter Ten

THE UNEXPECTED FORCE of Carse Boling's blows drove Jedrow to one knee. As he regained his feet, Jedrow picked up a half-gallon tin of sliced peaches. He hurled the heavy can at Carse's head. Carse ducked, but the can smashed him on the shoulder. The impact spun him and the tin landed in the center of the cook fire, scattering embers. Men were shouting. Riders, those that could be spared from the herd, spurred up.

Jedrow leaped and tried to wrap his thick arms about Carse, but the shorter man managed to twist away. As he did so, Carse sent the point of his elbow ripping across Jedrow's Adam's apple. Jedrow gave a hoarse cry at the pain. But before Carse could step back and level on him, Jedrow managed to get the fingers of both hands on Carse's belt. With his great strength Jedrow lifted the Coffin partner off his feet and dumped him headfirst to the ground.

As Carse fell back, the close-packed group of yelling riders broke apart. Jedrow closed and with the rowels of his spurs ripped Carse from right ankle to thigh. Carse cried out and could feel blood on his leg and knew he was lucky that the heavy denim of his pants had minimized the full effect of the sharpened rowels. Bleeding from his cuts, Carse moved crabwise across the ground. He escaped another attempt by Jedrow to use the spurs. Angered, shaky, he got to his feet, and Jedrow smashed him on the mouth. Carse swung hard and connected with a hard left under the heart that made Jedrow grunt. But Jedrow lunged and caught Carse in the chest with the tip of a shoulder. As Carse went to his knees, Jedrow tried to rake his face with the spurs. Carse got him by the right leg and spilled him. As Jedrow regained his feet, Carse was waiting, and hit him twice in the face.

Riders from other outfits were enlarging the crowd and there was a great cry of excitement every time a blow was struck. Even though they favored Carse, those that took a realistic view of the battle put their money on the big Jedrow, whose weight advantage and reach would grad-

64

ually wear down the shorter man, they were sure. There was no doubt of the outcome in their eyes.

Carse pursued his man relentlessly. He smashed at the heavy bone of Jedrow's face, his knuckles splitting the skin. Again Jedrow picked up a can of peaches and sent it whistling past Carse's face. Carse flung up an arm to deflect the missile. The blow spun him around. Before he could right himself, Jedrow had him about the waist and bore him to the ground. They squirmed and cursed and rolled from side to side, churning up the dust.

Bert Radich and his brother watched the fight, displaying none of the enthusiasm of the other onlookers. Ralph Shamley of Anchor cried, "Kill him, Carse!"

Carse managed to get his fingers entwined in Jedrow's long brown hair. He jerked Jedrow's head down, at the same time lifting his knee. Even from his awkward position on the ground, it was an effective blow. Carse heard Jedrow's cry of pain, felt the bones of the nose collapse under the point of his knee. Thoroughly aroused by what this big man was doing to Emily and Staggart and himself, Carse rocked Jedrow with lefts and rights. He got to his feet, breathing hard.

Johnny D'Orr yelled, "Finish him, Carse!"

"Don't let Jedrow get them spurs in your face!" Ben Smiley called.

Still squealing from the pain of his smashed nose, Jedrow rushed the Coffin partner. Carse fought him off, but took a blow in the pit of the stomach that doubled him up. Despite Jedrow's size, he moved with surprising ease.

Again Jedrow charged straight through Carse Boling's guard, ramming the crown of his skull into Carse's midriff. Carse went sprawling on his shoulder blades across the cook fire.

The fall stunned him and he felt himself jerked to his feet. Hands were slapping his back. He felt heat and knew his shirt was on fire.

"Wait'll I get the fire out!" Johnny D'Orr yelled at Jedrow.

Someone tore off the blazing shirt. Jedrow was not waiting. Sweeping out a big hand, he knocked Johnny D'Orr off his feet.

Before Carse could clear his head, Jedrow's fist caught him on the right temple. Carse looked up, seeing Jedrow towering above him. For a moment Carse did not realize that the blow that had set his head to ringing had knocked him off his feet. Then he saw the downsweep of Jedrow's spurred boot. Desperately he grabbed for the ankle. He missed. The spur hit the palm of his right hand, ripping the flesh. He clung to the spur and Jedrow staggered.

Because of his torn hand, it was painful for Carse to clench his right fist, but rage minimized the pain as he regained his feet. He slugged Jedrow. Carse's right cheekbone was laid bare. His shirt was torn off. There was a swelling at his right eye and along his jaw.

They fought grimly, silently. They stumbled over the dishpan, fell against the chuck wagon. Carse felt a thin edge of panic. No matter how hard he struck the man, his blows seemed to do only surface damage. Jedrow's thick legs were absorbing most of the punishment. With his eyes almost swollen shut, Jedrow bored in again, smashing down Carse's guard with sheer power. Jedrow's lips were cut.

The two men were locked together again, wrestling across the camp. The onlookers set up a great clamor. The crowd continued to grow. Only enough men to hold the herd were left on duty, and even these were standing up in their stirrups, trying to catch a glimpse of what they all sensed was a historic battle. This was the first excitement for most of them since shipping time last year.

Carse felt Jedrow lock hands behind his back and bend him backward. In desperattion Carse brought up his knee, but instead of taking Jedrow in the groin, it only brushed his thigh. Carse spat into Jedrow's face. Blinded momentarily, Jedrow relaxed the pressure of his powerful arms slightly and Carse twisted free. Without waiting for Jedrow to wipe the spittle from his eyes, he struck.

Still smearing a forearm across his eyes, Jedrow bared his torn lips and with a cry of rage rushed his man. Carse kicked him hard in the stomach. This slowed Jedrow and Carse hit him twice in the face with all his strength.

Jedrow shook his head and came on. Carse felt his panic increase. His head still buzzed from the vicious clout Jedrow had given him on the temple earlier in the fight. Although Jedrow was marked from the savage mauling, he apparently had not been slowed. There seemed to be no limit to the man's endurance.

Carse was suddenly aware that the crowd no longer yelled. The men seemed to sense what he already knew:

that unless he ended this quickly, Jedrow would eventually wear him down and use the spurs.

Again Jedrow tried to get those murderous arms about his body so as to bear him to the ground. Carse got away from him. He kept his eyes on the point of Jedrow's heavy chin. The chin was cleft and there was an ugly bruise on the right side. Carse watched the cleft, his target, right fist cocked. He hit Jedrow with his left, but Jedrow had the reach, and as Carse came in he rocked his adversary with two smashes to the head. Carse reeled, spitting blood.

A growing horror touched him as another blow caught him on the forehead. As his knees buckled he saw the ground tilt sharply. For an instant he thought he was going down. Instinctively he wanted to grab Jedrow and hang on, anything to keep those fists from banging him in the face. Summoning all his will power, he forced his vision to clear. He watched his target.

In his eagerness, thinking Carse was hurt, Jedrow crowded close.

It seemed to Carse that Jedrow's cleft chin was pushed squarely into his own upswinging right fist. The shock of the blow jarred him. Jedrow's eyes crossed and the big man fell forward as if chopped off at the knees. He lay face down, making strangling sounds. One of the men finally turned him over on his back. Dust had clogged his nostrils. Jedrow fought for breath.

Johnny D'Orr, white with worry, showed his relief. "It was like you hit him with an anvil, Carse."

Old Ben Smiley exclaimed, "I never did see Carse hit him! It was sure quick!" The old cook was grinning happily. "The next thing I knowed, Jedrow was flat."

Wearily Carse stepped over the fallen man. He jerked Jedrow's gun from its holster and unloaded it. He flung the shells across the campground, then returned the gun to the holster. He saw Jedrow's eyes watching him, thin strips of green through the puffiness.

Carse sank to the ground, his back to a wheel of the chuck wagon. Somebody gave him some coffee laced with whisky. He drank it gratefully.

Jedrow finally got to his feet and glared at the silent crowd of men. Then his gaze settled on Carse. For a moment he stood there, then without a word he stumbled to his horse and rode out.

"I hope we've seen the last of him," Johnny D'Orr said.

Carse made no comment. As soon as he could he washed the blood off his face. His head ached. When Ben Smiley banged his iron bar on the triangle there seemed to be little appetite. Men could talk of nothing but the momentous fight.

Ben Smiley said, "Some of these youngsters will be telling their grandchildren about this fight, Carse. Yep, they'll tell of the day Carse Boling whipped the biggest man that ever stepped across the Dakota line."

Johnny D'Orr spat on the ground. "I should have shot the son-of-a-bitch the day he said he didn't like bunking with an Indian."

Johnny started away and Carse limped after him. "Forget it, Johnny," he warned. "Stay away from Jedrow. From now on he's going to be dangerous. Don't you try to prove anything by taking a gun to him."

Johnny said, "I was only fooling." But his dark eyes were bright and hard.

They finished roundup at the end of the week. Carse, still shaky from the fight, shook hands with the other owners and their riders.

Bert Radich said, "You was born lucky, Carse. I'll lay a hundred dollars to a hole in your hat you couldn't whip Jedrow again."

"There'd be no point in trying," Carse told him. "Next time I'll split his skull with a bullet."

The following morning Carse started 2,500 head of Coffin beef toward the Missouri and Bellfontaine. He made the drive leisurely, so the cattle would not lose too much weight.

Staggart finally met them on the trail. He had stayed in town. He seemed thinned down and harassed. "I hear you couldn't keep off Jedrow's neck."

Carse said angrily, "You act like it was my fault."

Staggart softened a little. "The whole town's heard about the fight. Sheriff Alcorte sent me out to warn you he won't stand for no trouble between you and Jedrow in town. You're to check your gun like everybody else."

"Remember to tell that to Jedrow."

Staggart brightened. "I got the preacher lined up so's you and Margretha can get married."

"I'll talk about that later," Carse said. "I've got to get this herd to Bellfontaine."

Staggart gave him an ugly glance. "I ain't been a virtuous man myself, Carse. But I won't stand for no monkeying with my kin. If you've touched that girl, you'll marry her."

"Stag, I thought I knew you, but seven years has taught me nothing. I don't know you at all." Carse still had a cut on his right cheek and his mouth was bruised, but the swelling had gone down on his jaws. "You should have taken a gun to Jedrow for the talk he's spread about Emily. The way you're acting just doesn't make any sense at all."

Staggart said, "I'm plumb sorry I thought there was something between you and Em."

Carse said, "Ever hear of a man named Martin from Mogollon, New Mexico?"

Staggart's mouth fell open. He looked wildly about, but the riders pushing the herd were some distance away. "Where'd you hear that name?" he cried.

"I went through Jedrow's trunk. I found a clipping about a man by that name who escaped a hanging. I also found a photograph of Jedrow and Kellerway."

Staggart's face was white. "Carse, I—"

"No wonder you hated to have anybody call you Martin. You changed your name when you came here. Where'd you get Staggart?"

"My mother's maiden name."

"You could have saved everybody trouble if you'd spoken out before this, Stag. You've brought nothing but grief to Emily. Can't you see that somebody's tried to stir up trouble between you and me over Emily? They know you're jealous and you've got a pretty wife younger than you. They thought you'd get mad enough to take a gun, and either you'd kill me or I'd kill you. Either way, whoever is behind this would have had one of us out of the way. If you died, then they'd only have to 'bush me, then move in on Emily. If I died—well, they'd use whatever they're holding over your head to get the rest of Coffin. With me out of the way, they figured there'd be nobody left to stick up for you. Except Johnny, of course."

Staggart's mouth trembled. "He hates my guts."

"He'd fight to save Coffin for Emily, if not for you."

Staggart was gray under his mustache. "I asked you to wait till after we shipped. I begged you to. And you had to go mix with Jedrow just over a damn cutting horse."

Carse said, "I never knew before you were too gutless

to face up to something. Face up to Jedrow and Keller-way and whoever else is bleeding you. Face up and be the man I used to know."

Staggart straightened his shoulders. "We'll talk about this after we sell the herd." He spoke coldly. "See you in Bellfontaine."

Chapter Eleven

CARSE BOLING sent the herd across the Missouri in bunches of two hundred. He picked a place where in other days the buffalo had crossed and worn the approaches smooth with their hoofs. For the buffalo had instinctively known where the currents were less treacherous and where there was no quicksand. Carse had horses and riders that were good swimmers. The riders shucked down to their red underwear, and, with their horses unhampered by saddles, they kept the cattle streaming across the river.

Bellfontaine looked different than it had on Carse's last visit. As they approached they could hear a clamor of activity: engines dragging empty cattle cars into sidings; other engines on the main line with beef trains; pens along the tracks jammed with cattle; herds bedded down on the flats beyond the town. Carse cautioned his men about Sheriff Luke Alcorte's no-gun ruling.

Johnny D'Orr said, "What if Jedrow's in town?"

"He'll come under the same rule. If he still wants trouble, we can settle it after the cattle are shipped."

Carse pushed the herd to the bed ground always used by Coffin. Then he decided to look around for the Archer packing-house representative and see how the beef market looked for the year.

Johnny D'Orr said, "Who's going to Chi this year? You or Stag?"

"Me," Carse said, and wanted to add that he would never return to Dakota. He smiled at Johnny. Someday maybe he would send for him. It would do Johnny good to get away from Coffin. Stag didn't like him and he was a constant worry to Emily.

Before Carse could look for the Archer rep, Stag, wearing a new black suit, drove up in a hired buggy. With him was Paul Kellerway, dapper, well dressed. Between the two men was Allison Kellerway. She wore a small brown hat and a brown dress tight at the sleeves. Her brown eyes were large as she watched Carse Boling.

Kellerway smiled and waved a hand at the herd. "Looks like you've got prime beef there, Boling. Nice work."

71

Carse made no comment. He stood, hat in hand, watching Staggart. The rancher smoked a cigar and seemed to be taking unusually large draughts of smoke and expelling it from a corner of his mouth.

Obviously ill at ease, Staggart said, "Tell the crew I'll be in Goodfellow's at four o'clock to pay off."

Carse frowned. "But the herd isn't even sold yet. You don't pay till we have the money."

Staggart said, without looking at him, "It's sold. Kellerway bought it."

Kellerway wore a narrow-brimmed black hat. His shirt was spotless and made Carse all the more conscious of his own rough clothing.

"Staggart drives a hard bargain," Kellerway said with his warm smile. "But I hope to resell at a profit."

Staggart lifted the reins. "See you at Goodfellow's."

Kellerway said, "I'll have my own men take over the herd, Boling." The buggy moved off toward town.

Carse saw Allison Kellerway turn and look back at him, one hand holding her small hat because of the stiff breeze. He thought, How can such a pretty girl have such a skunk for a brother? Or maybe they're both of the same stripe.

He gathered the Coffin hands around him and told them they would be getting their money earlier than expected. This brought whoops of joy. The big outfits such as Coffin did not pay from spring roundup until shipping time. After the herd was sold, the men received their money in one lump.

When Kellerway's crew arrived to take charge of the herd, Carse rode uptown with his men to Ekert's Livery. There Ekert, bearded and querulous, reminded them to leave their guns. They hung their belts on pegs in the saddle room.

There was a jam of traffic on the streets, buggies, wagons, freighters, horsemen. Carse had worn a gun so much recently that he felt odd without the accustomed weight dragging at his belt. He felt the rising excitement of the men that walked with him. Their eyes glistened and one of them waved at a smiling woman wearing a red silk dress. "Later, honey, when I get my pay," the hand shouted good-naturedly. And the woman turned back into the crowd and directed her smile elsewhere.

The lank, mustached Sheriff Alcorte met Carse and Johnny on the walk. The rest of the crew moved on to

Goodfellow's, where tabs could be signed until they received their pay.

"Things ought to be peaceful this year, with no guns," Alcorte said. And when Carse agreed, the Sheriff added, "I've got Jedrow's word that he won't seek trouble unless you start it."

"So."

"Have I got your word?"

"Yeah, you've got my word."

The Sheriff studied Carse Boling's tight brown face to detect any reservation. Satisfied, Alcorte said, "Jedrow's going to be around town for a spell. He's taken a job with Paul Kellerway."

Carse gave a short laugh. "If you ask me, they've always been working together."

Alcorte's sparse brows arched. "I don't like Jedrow much, but Kellerway is an asset to this town. He's bringing business here. Got lots of connections with Chicago and Kansas City firms."

"That so?"

"And of course he's got a pretty sister." The Sheriff grinned. "Too bad you're spoken for. You might give her a whirl."

"Just where did you get the idea I'm spoken for?"

"You're marrying Staggart's niece Saturday, aren't you? Everybody knows about it." When Carse said nothing, the Sheriff said uneasily, "It's true, ain't it?"

Carse said, "The more I'm here, the less I like this country. Too many people like Jedrow and Kellerway."

"Let me tell you this," Alcorte said. "Bert Radich was saying only yesterday that Paul Kellerway is a fine fella. Bert kind of wants him to succeed here."

Carse said, "And if the Radich brothers tell you an idea, you suck it dry. I guess everybody knows they practically elect you every term."

As the Sheriff turned red, Johnny D'Orr said, "Why don't you worry about important things, Sheriff? Such as whether I could buy a drink of whisky at Oren Goodfellow's without the Army or a U.S. marshal finding out. But I wouldn't want Oren to get in trouble for selling a drink to a damn Indian like me."

The Sheriff stalked off through the crowd.

Carse said, "Johnny, you act like Ben Smiley always says—with a burr up your butt."

They walked together to Si Gorman's.

Johnny gave a bitter laugh. "Now if I was a scalping Indian, that hair of Kellerway's would look nice at my belt. Just enough gray in it."

Carse gave Johnny D'Orr a hard look. "No wonder Emily loses sleep over you. Maybe one of these days you and me ought to clear out of here."

"It ain't me Emily worries about," Johnny said, and gave Carse an odd smile.

They had to wait their turn because of the crowd. Finally they saw Gorman's bald head moving their way. The old merchant commented on the lack of guns in town. "I hope Alcorte can make it stick," Gorman said. "But sometimes I think he's all brag and no guts."

"He's a good enough sheriff," Carse said.

"Alcorte is mighty friendly with Paul Kellerway," Gorman said softly.

"Is that a crime?"

"No, but you watch out that Staggart doesn't get himself hung up on Kellerway's fence."

Johnny D'Orr's dark young face tightened. "He won't. Not while I'm around. Staggart won't sell out my sister."

Carse gripped the younger man's arm. "Shut up, Johnny. Emily can handle her own affairs."

Johnny shook off Carse's hand. "I'll be around to see that she handles them."

"Couple of suits of Updegraft's," Carse said to Gorman, "and a new shirt."

"Same for me," Johnny told the merchant. "But red's a hell of a color for an Indian." He tried to laugh.

Gorman failed to catch the irony in Johnny's tone. "Underwear comes only in one color. Sorry, Johnny."

As they went out into the hot sunlight they heard a blare of brassy music from the Red Devil Dance Hall. A banner across the front said: "35 Girls 35. $1 A Dance."

Men were crowding into the doorway.

Carse reflected: "The Kansas City women have arrived."

Johnny said slyly, "Wonder what Big Min's got at her place this year."

"Why don't you find out?"

"I leave that sort of thing to Stag."

Carse was silent as they crossed the street, their purchases under their arms. As they neared Dave Shell's barbershop, Johnny said, "If you were married to Emily, would you go off to Big Min's?"

Carse frowned, threading his way between an L & E Freighter and Ralph Shamley's town wagon. "Depends on the man," Carse said thoughtfully, remembering his talk with Big Min. "Maybe I'd do it if I had as much on my mind as Stag has. Don't condemn him too much, Johnny."

"Hell, you condemn him yourself. I overheard you and him arguing the other day. You told him to be a man and speak out against Jedrow."

Carse did not wish to carry the discussion further. They entered Shell's barbershop, and while they waited their turns at the bath, they got their hair trimmed and had a shave.

Dave Shell said, "I hear Staggart sold the herd to Kellerway this year."

"Yeah," Carse said.

"I thought Staggart always did business with Archer. You have anything to say about selling to Kellerway?"

"Not a damn thing, Dave," Carse admitted.

The room fell silent, and Johnny, in the adjoining barber chair, said softly, "You're Stag's partner when it comes to doing most of the work, but when it comes time to hire a man like Jedrow or sell beef, you don't count worth a damn in his eyes."

"I'll settle with Stag," Carse said, "after he pays off the men. I aim to have a good long talk with him."

They had their shave and haircut and then, because Carse wanted to get Johnny's mind off Staggart, he removed a coin from his pocket. "Flip you to see who gets first in the bathtub." When Johnny nodded, Carse threw the coin into the air and caught it. Johnny won.

Johnny grinned. "Your luck is bad today, Carse."

Looking back on the moment later, Carse knew that Johnny had been very wrong. It was Johnny's luck that was bad. Later, he wondered what fate had guided that coin flashing upward into the shaft of sunlight pouring through Shell's window, and made it fall so that Johnny D'Orr was first in the zinc-lined tub.

When Johnny went to take his bath, Carse listened to the talk of beef and of shipping. There was excitement in the crowded shop, for these were the weeks when Bellfontaine roused to the clamor of those that sought her favors. Men had money in their pockets and there was talk of big plans for the winter. The buying of a prize bull, ordering stuff from the mail-order house. Dreams in the air.

And also in the air was a generous odor of Forest Night, the talc that came in a large can and had the painting of a nymph in a forest on its front. Dave Shell gave his customers a generous sprinkling after each shave. Carse took a chair.

"Wish I could have seen you bust Sam Jedrow," one of the men commented.

Carse said, "I was lucky. His chin just happened to get in the way of my fist."

Some of the men laughed. One of them said, "The way I hear it, you must have hit him with a mattock handle."

Johnny D'Orr finally came out of the bathroom, scrubbed and wearing his new shirt. "See you at Good-fellow's," Johnny told Carse.

A man said, "If Oren goes selling whisky to you, Johnny, they'll have him locked up in the stockade at the fort."

Johnny said, "My grandpa was an Oglala chief. He's likely run his war lance through the breastbone of more than one loud talker like you." He went out, slamming the door.

The man who had spoken was red-faced. "Hell, I was only joking."

Carse got up, his bundle under his arm. "Keep joking like that through the winter, friend, and you're liable to meet somebody who can't take a joke. We'd hate to miss you next shipping time."

In the bathroom Shell's helper poured buckets of hot water that had been heating over a fire in the yard.

When the tub was filled, Carse stripped. He wadded up his old suit of red underwear and hurled it out the rear door into the yard, adding to a generous pile of garments discarded by those who had previously occupied the bathroom this day. It was an annual ritual.

He scrubbed and soaked in the tub until he had used up the time Shell allotted to each bather. Leisurely he dressed. He had just gone into the shop and paid Shell when he heard the shot.

Men left their chairs and crowded around the window, peering up the street. A shot was not uncommon in Bellfontaine, but the fact that by official decree all guns were to be checked did make it unusual for this year.

Carse saw old Ben Smiley coming rapidly along the

street, skirting traffic that had halted at the gun blast. The old cook moved as fast as his crippled leg would allow.

"Carse!" the old man shouted.

A feeling of apprehension touched Carse and he stepped outside. The cook's face was gray. He looked at Carse. "It's Johnny," Ben Smiley said. "Oh, God, the bullet caught him right in the face. It's awful, Carse. Awful."

Aware of men, speechless, crowding around him, Carse said, "Ben, who did it?"

"Sam Jedrow."

Chapter Twelve

WHEN STAGGART drove away from the Coffin bed grounds he let Paul Kellerway and his sister off at the small white house they had taken at the edge of town. Kellerway said, "Your partner doesn't seem to like it that you did business with me."

Staggart said heavily, "I'll explain to him."

"I hope you do," Kellerway said, smiling. "I don't want Allison to think there was anything underhanded in the transaction." He transferred his smile to his half sister. "There wasn't anything underhanded, was there, Staggart?"

"Of course not," Staggart said, but he did not look at Kellerway.

He drove uptown and left the buggy at Ekert's. He entered the crowded Goodfellow saloon. He caught sight of his reflection in the backbar mirror and did not like the face that stared back at him. The face shamed him. He felt a moment of panic as he wondered if the world he had so carefully built here was beginning to break up.

In this country he was a power. Save for the Radich brothers, there was no one with more power. He had a pretty wife. Every year he sold at least 2,500 head of beef. Every year but this one. His only expenses were the salaries he paid and the feeding of his men. Despite these reassurances, he felt the breath of a cold wind down his back.

He passed the time of day with Bert Radich. Then he saw Sam Jedrow enter the saloon. The big man's Chihuahua spurs made an ugly chiming sound. The only satisfaction Staggart had experienced so far this day was seeing Jedrow's face still marked from Carse Boling's fists. Jedrow's nose was still swollen and it altered the man's facial expression. Jedrow wore gray pants and a new hat. And despite the heat he wore a leather jacket.

He came down the bar and nodded at Staggart. "A man lookin' as sour as you do ought to have a drink," Jedrow told him.

Staggart shook his head. "I never drink till the crew is

paid off." Anxious to get away from Jedrow, he moved to the green-topped poker table that Oren Goodfellow always reserved for the afternoon when Staggart paid off his men.

Goodfellow came up, smoothing his hair across his balding dome. He wanted to know how much money Stag would need from the bank.

Staggart opened his time book. He owed his regular hands for all the months since spring roundup. The rest of the hands he owed only for the time they had worked during the roundup. He told Goodfellow he would need roughly $4,500.

Presently Goodfellow and two of his men returned from the bank with a heavy iron box. This was placed beside Staggart's chair at the poker table. Staggart lit a cigar with a hand that shook slightly. He had bathed and his hair and mustache were trimmed. He smelled of Forest Night talc.

A few of the extra hands who had been drinking at the bar now stepped up. Staggart paid them off and checked their names out of the book. From then on business at the Coffin table was brisk. The regular hands who had run a bill at Goodfellow's paid off and then started paying cash for their drinks. Within a matter of hours some of them would be running tabs again. A lot of them roared down the block to the Red Devil, where they would dance with the Kansas City women for a dollar. Others went to Big Min's.

Jedrow had gone to a roulette layout and promptly lost twenty-five dollars. He sauntered up to the Coffin table, hat pushed back from the V of hair low on his forehead. Because there were men present who had witnessed his defeat at the hands of Staggart's partner, Jedrow seemed more belligerent than usual, as if he were defying anyone to comment on the condition of his face. Those in the saloon were careful not to look at him openly as he passed, but behind his back some of them winked and smiled.

Jedrow had a drink and then another. Everyone gave him room. He towered over every other man in the place.

The payoff of the Coffin hands was proceeding briskly when Johnny D'Orr, his young dark face embittered, entered the saloon. He spoke to Oren Goodfellow.

Jedrow said loudly, "Goodfellow, don't you know it's against federal law to sell whisky to an Indian?"

Goodfellow, who was helping out behind his bar, cast a worried glance at the taut Johnny D'Orr. "I don't figure Johnny for an Indian. But some folks might. Just to be on the safe side, he drinks nothing but Aquarius water. Right, Johnny?"

Johnny took the bottle of mineral water Goodfellow passed to him over the bar. Johnny's black eyes were hard against Jedrow's bruised face.

Johnny said, "The whipping Carse Boling gave you didn't make you any easier to get along with."

There was a sudden quiet at the end of the bar where Jedrow stood balanced on the toes of his boots.

Staggart said, "That's enough, Johnny!" He sat stiffly in the chair at the poker table. The men waiting to be paid were looking from Johnny to Sam Jedrow.

Johnny D'Orr said, "Tell Jedrow it's enough. I didn't start it. Besides, he don't work any more for Coffin. Carse fired him. So why do you tell me it's enough?"

When Johnny had his second bottle of mineral water Jedrow said to the grim line of Coffin riders in the pay line, "A man's hair don't rest easy with a drunk Indian at his back. Good thing he's not drinking hard liquor."

Johnny gripped the bottle as if to use it as a club. He caught sight of Staggart at the table and the rancher shot him such a look of appeal that Johnny put the bottle back.

Staggart said, "Jedrow, leave him alone."

Staggart spoke so softly that only Jedrow and the men in line heard what he said through the clamor in the big saloon.

Jedrow shifted his feet so that the rowels of his spurs rattled against the floor. "Staggart, you talk pretty tough." There was a strained silence and on some of the faces there was a measure of pity for what Staggart was taking from the big man. Most of the crowd, however, was noisily celebrating the end of roundup and paying little attention.

Staggart said gruffly, "You oughtn't to pick on Johnny." Staggart looked up from his time book and into the questioning eyes of the men in line. Something snapped in him and he slammed a fist on the table so hard that a stack of gold coins toppled over.

"I run Coffin!" he shouted. "I hire and I fire. I got the most money in the ranch. I say who stays and who leaves. Not Carse Boling!"

None of those in line commented. They shifted restlessly and some of them exchanged glances. After a moment, as if knowing he had lost some stature here by the outburst, he mopped his forehead with a bandanna. He knew Carse had friends in this saloon and they would resent the way he had spoken.

When he resumed paying off, old Ben Smiley was next in line. Staggart tried to appear the jovial rancher of other years. He pushed some coins at Smiley and put a check mark opposite the cook's name. "It's a wonder the boys ain't got holes in their guts from eating that swill you call grub." Staggart laughed with false heartiness. He lost some of his humor as he glanced at Smiley's grave face. He pushed another coin at Smiley and said, "Five extra, Ben. You're the best cook I ever had."

Smiley picked up the extra coin and said, "Thanks, Mr. Staggart." He did not smile.

Staggart seemed to explode. "Smiley, you don't have to look sour as a gravedigger. What's eatin' you? I do something you don't like?" he cursed. "It's the first time you ever called me Mr. Staggart."

"I just figure a man ought to stick up for his partner, that's all. You didn't." Ben Smiley limped away from the pay table, jingling the coins in his pocket.

Staggart sat with his mouth open, a flush stealing over his freshly shaved cheeks. Had one of the ranch firebrands spoken out as the cook had done, Staggart would have fired the man on the spot. But this had been the usually mild old cook, and his words had caught Staggart off guard.

Goodfellow said to some of the crowd around his end of the bar, "If this had been last year, with the boys wearing their guns, somebody would be shot up about now." He sighed with obvious relief.

To cover his anger and embarrassment at being reprimanded by his cook in front of the crowd, Staggart fumbled more coins from the big iron box beside his chair. Mixed in with the coins in the box was a loaded .45. Sheriff Alcorte had deemed it advisable that Staggart have the means to defend himself in the event that some outsiders, ignoring the gun ban in Bellfontaine, might ride in and try to take over the Coffin payroll. Mechanically Staggart paid off his men. He chewed an unlighted cigar and did not even look up when the men announced their names. At his elbow was a quart of whisky, something no one had ever seen there before the payoff was complete. He drank savagely, cursing this country, forgetting that it had been good to him.

He thought of how he had first come here ten years ago. Henri D'Orr had kept the Indians off his neck, and this enabled him to appropriate land with the best water and run his cattle unmolested. Henri D'Orr was married to a chief's daughter. D'Orr had lived to educate his children. In Emily's case it had been good, but not so for Johnny. Johnny was rebellious, and the books his father had given him to read only intensified his awareness that in this country he was not always accepted. Not being able to stand in Goodfellow's saloon and drink with the others rankled most of all. Once Johnny had drunk a pint at one sitting and Carse Boling had said, "It's not the whisky an Indian drinks that makes him wild. It's the way he drinks. Save a little for the next day."

But the drunkenness and the loss of memory that followed it frightened Johnny D'Orr, and he was thoroughly convinced that this legend of the Indian and whisky was fact. He never touched it again.

Sam Jedrow got up from a monte game, cursing his bad luck. He pushed his way through the crowd to Staggart's table.

He bent over and put his hand in the iron box and came up with a handful of coins. Staggart had turned instinctively when, from the corner of his eye, he saw somebody reach into the box. The rancher twisted on the chair, then choked off an oath when he saw who it was standing there.

The line of Coffin riders was strangely silent and watchful. It seemed incredible that Staggart was allowing this brazen action.

Jedrow said carelessly, "As long as you say I'm still on the Coffin payroll, make me out an I.O.U. for three hundred dollars." He smiled coldly.

Before the stricken Staggart could write out the I.O.U. for Jedrow's signature, Johnny D'Orr burst up to the table, his black eyes flaming in his Indian face.

"Stag, have you gone crazy?" he demanded.

Staggart put the palms of both hands on the table as if to rise. "This ain't your business," he said through his teeth.

"It's Emily's business if you figure to give Coffin away. And that makes it my business!"

Staggart swallowed. "I'll explain to Emily. But I sure, as hell don't have to explain to her brother."

"By God, Stag, you've lost your senses!" Johnny D'Orr also put his hand into the box, and when he brought it out again he was holding the .45. There was a scramble and a shout: "He's got Staggart's gun!"

Johnny eyed the rigid Sam Jedrow. "Stag would bust the head of any other man who did what you just did. Why you're so special I can't figure." He cocked the revolver. "Put the money back."

Jedrow looked at the .45, then lifted his eyes to Johnny's face. "You crazy damn Indian," he said.

"Put it back!" Johnny cried.

"Go to hell." Jedrow turned his back and started away.

Johnny lifted the gun and Staggart cried out in an anguished voice: "No, Johnny. He ain't got a gun. Kill him and you'll hang sure!"

The wisdom of this got through Johnny's rage and cooled it somewhat. Plainly not knowing how he could stop the big man stalking away without shooting him, Johnny let the barrel of the .45 sag.

Jedrow, who had moved in such a way as to have Johnny's reflection constantly in view in the backbar mirror, gave a small hard smile. He turned quickly. There was a powder flash and an explosion as he extended his right hand, and the lower part of Johnny's face disappeared.

Chapter Thirteen

Carse Boling stood for a moment in the street, watching Ben Smiley sag against the bar of the hitch rail and retch after he had told his tale. A crowd had gathered and there were men peering from the barbershop window, one of them with lather on his cheeks. An unnatural quiet had descended upon Bellfontaine.

Dave Shell came out of his shop, shielding his eyes against the sun and looking up Chicago Street toward the knot of men that had formed about the front doors of Oren Goodfellow's saloon.

Shell said, "How could Johnny get shot when all the guns was supposed to be checked?"

"It's a damn certainty," Carse said, "somebody had a gun." He was recovering from his first shock. Not long ago it had been Hank Peavey. Now it was Johnny D'Orr. He went over and put a hand on Ben Smiley's shoulder. "Easy, Ben. Easy."

Then he walked purposefully up the street, turning into Ekert's. In the harness room he got his gun and then he moved on to Goodfellow's. There was an odd silence in the place as Carse entered. Sheriff Alcorte was just about to lower an Indian blanket over Johnny D'Orr's body. Carse thought: I hope Emily doesn't want to look at her brother before we bury him.

At the Coffin table Staggart sat with his chin on his breastbone, clutching a bottle of whisky.

Carse said into the quiet, "What happened, Stag?"

Staggart sat as if in a daze. Sheriff Alcorte spoke up nervously. "Johnny pulled a gun on Sam Jedrow." The Sheriff spread his hands. "It was self-defense."

Carse looked across the bar at Oren Goodfellow's pale face. "What do you say, Oren?"

"Johnny had a gun. He took it out of Stag's money box."

"And where did Jedrow get his gun?" Carse asked the Sheriff in a tight voice. "I thought every gun was to be checked at the livery."

"I can't watch everybody," Alcorte snapped. "Anyhow,

84

if Jedrow hadn't had a gun, Johnny would have killed him." He smeared a hand across his moist forehead. "Maybe better that Johnny got it this way. If he shot Jedrow in the back, I'd be the one to hang him."

There was a tense silence. Ranged along the bar were the Radich brothers. Bert said, "Alcorte is only trying to do his duty, Carse. Why don't you let him handle this?"

The slight Ardo Radich said, "Bert's right. Bert sure is right."

"Shut up, Ardo," Carse said quietly. "Sometimes you remind me of a mockingbird."

Ardo's face got red, but Bert only laughed and put a match to a cigar.

Alcorte turned to the hard-eyed Ed Lopart and Art Quince, who lounged against the far wall. Quince avoided Carse's eyes.

Alcorte said, "You boys saw it happen. Do you think Johnny aimed to shoot Jedrow in the back?"

"That's what he figured to do," Ed Lopart said in his unemotional voice. He turned his face with the spike beard on Quince. "Ain't that right, Art?"

Quince shrugged and looked down at the floor. "If Jedrow hadn't shook a gun out of the sleeve of his leather jacket, Johnny would have killed him."

Carse looked around the tense, crowded barroom. He pointed out the fact that not a man was wearing a coat because of the heat. "Jedrow was wearing a leather jacket. He'd fry in the heat just so he'd be able to wear a derringer up his sleeve." He turned on Stag. "That means that Jedrow came here with one intention: to get Johnny in a fight and kill him."

"No," Staggart said drunkenly.

Carse advanced to the poker table and the big rancher straightened up in the chair. Staggart licked at his mustache. "Now see here, Carse. I feel bad enough about Johnny without you makin' it worse."

Carse said, "You and Luke Alcorte came out of the same bucket. When somebody pins you to the wall you start talking tough."

Alcorte said, "I don't have to take that kind of talk."

Carse laughed coldly. "No, you don't, Luke. You don't have to take it at all. I'm just boiling because a kid was murdered. But I should shake Jedrow's hand, I suppose."

"It wasn't murder," Alcorte cried.

Carse went on as if the Sheriff had not spoken. "Instead of talking tough to Sam Jedrow, you talk tough to me."

Staggart swayed a little in the chair as he tried to stiffen his shoulders. "Johnny's been asking for trouble for years. You know that."

"Only because he was sensitive. None of you would let him forget he was part Oglala. It seems a small thing to us, maybe, but Johnny took it to heart because he couldn't stand up at the bar and drink whisky with the rest of us. And it wasn't altogether that Oren wouldn't sell to him. It was because Johnny believed he couldn't drink. That he was enough Indian so that whisky made him crazy. He felt apart from the rest of us. But instead of making it easier for him, every time he stepped into this saloon somebody remarked about him taking a scalp knife if he got a drink of whisky. It was enough to make any man a little wild." Carse looked around the barroom, seeing the faces, some of them ashamed now.

Then his gaze fell on Staggart. "I'll tell you who really killed Johnny. It was you, Stag. You let Jedrow come to Coffin and do as he pleased. You let him get Johnny into a corner. You're the one, Stag. Jedrow planned to get Johnny, to get him out of the way. He would try for me next. And then you. Then only Emily would be left."

He stepped forward and the flat of his right hand crashed against Staggart's face. The rancher fell sideways out of the chair. Staggart struck the floor, blinking his eyes. He seemed dazed. Then his face hardened as the drunken paralysis seemed to leave. He put a hand toward the open money box next to the table where he lay. On top of the coins was the .45 that Johnny had taken.

Carse said, "Stag, if you think I did wrong, pick up that gun. I'll give you a chance to use it."

He stepped back and waited. There was a scuffle of boots as men broke away from them.

Oren Goodfellow said, "Stop them, Alcorte. No matter what's happened, they're partners. They've been friends. We've had enough killing for one day."

Alcorte said in his official voice, "Hold it, Carse."

At last Staggart got shakily to his feet. He rubbed the side of his face, red from Carse's hand. "Damn you," Stag muttered. "There was no need to lay a hand on me."

Deliberately Carse turned his back and started for the

door. Sheriff Alcorte blocked him. "Now see here, Carse. We don't want any more trouble. You take off that gun and gave it to me."

Carse said, "Where's Jedrow?"

Alcorte looked more harassed than usual. "I sent Jedrow away until you get a chance to simmer down. I won't stand for any more shooting in this town."

"You're a little late," Carse said, and pushed the Sheriff from the door and went outside. There was a crowd on the veranda that overflowed to the walk and into the street. Eyes watched him questioningly.

"Go get him, Carse," a man cried. "You whipped him once with your fists. You can do it again with a gun."

Carse pushed his way through the crowd and moved to the opposite side of the street. Women called shrilly to their offspring and hurried them out of possible danger. Girls from the Red Devil had come onto the walk to peer at Carse and talk together excitedly. Traffic still had not moved on Chicago Street since the blast of Jedrow's derringer.

Carse climbed the stairs to Paul Kellerway's office. Drawing his gun, he tried the door. It was locked. He kicked it open and then stepped aside. Peering around the shattered doorframe, he saw that the office was empty.

Sheriff Alcorte had come to the foot of the stairs. "Kellerway had nothin' to do with Johnny getting killed. You got no right to bust in a man's door!"

Carse ignored him and walked to Ekert's. Small boys tagged along, excitement on their shining faces. Carse got his horse saddled while men jammed the wide stable doorway, speculating on his next move.

Old Ben Smiley elbowed his way into the livery. "Alcorte's swearing in six deputies, Carse. He's going to lock you up till you cool off."

"It'll be forty years before I cool off."

He mounted, and Ekert, standing in his office doorway, said, "Johnny was a good kid."

"Paul Kellerway has a house in town. Where is it?"

"The old Logan place," Ekert said.

Carse rode out the back way, through the wagon yard. He let himself out a gate, turned and locked it. He crossed vacant lots. At the far end of a side street he saw a neat white house in a grove of cottonwoods. The house was set far back from the street behind a picket fence. Instead of dismounting and going on foot along the walk, Carse jumped his horse over the fence and rode up to the porch.

Allie Kellerway, who had been sitting on the porch, rose, white-faced. "Do you always ride your horse through a flower bed when you come calling?"

He did not look down at the damage the hoofs of his horse had done to some greenery. "Where's your brother?" he demanded.

She had come to the edge of the porch, her face regaining some of its color. "Paul left town for a few days." Her brown eyes watched him.

"Where's Sam Jedrow?"

"I—I don't know." She wore a dress of some thin material. It clung to her, and had he not been so pressured with this day's business, he would have appreciated her smoothly curved figure.

He stepped down and climbed the steps. "Maybe I believe you," he said. "But I'm not taking a chance."

He went into the house, shouting, "Jedrow! Kellerway!"

She followed him in and said indignantly, "You can't enter a person's home this way!"

"I want Jedrow."

"I told you I haven't seen him."

"Mind if I look to make sure?"

"Yes, I mind very much!"

The light was dim in the parlor. He saw worn furniture and a Franklin stove. As he started along the hallway she clutched at his arm, but he shook her off. When she followed he caught her by the elbows and swung her aside.

She kicked at him. When she tried to claw him he said, "You she-cat!"

He moved on, inspecting the first of two bedrooms. There were lacy curtains at the window. The second room had a masculine plainness and there was a half-smoked cigar on the stand beside the bed. This he guessed was her brother's room.

The rest of the house was also empty. He returned to the parlor, where she sat on the arm of a chair, angrily swinging her foot.

"Mr. Boling, I think you're the most brazen individual it has ever been my misfortune to meet."

"I could say the same thing about some other people. Your brother and Jedrow." He gave her a hard look. "There was a man killed uptown. Sam Jedrow killed him."

She crossed both hands over her breasts. "I heard a shot," she said. "Who was killed?"

"Johnny D'Orr. Emily Staggart's brother."

She looked away. "You believe my brother had something to do with it. Is that why you came here?"

"Jedrow works for your brother."

She got to her feet, tall and tense. "I—I've never liked Jedrow." Her eyes were filled with compassion. "Would I be of any comfort to Mrs. Staggart?"

"Womenfolks are always welcome at a time like this."

"Then I'll go to Coffin."

Suddenly he knew where his first duty lay: to Emily. Jedrow and Kellerway could wait. "I'm taking Johnny to Coffin. You can go with me if you like."

He went to the porch while she changed her clothes. Presently she reappeared dressed in a work shirt and Levis that fitted her snugly. She had taken down her luxuriant hair and tied it in back with a ribbon. She looked as she had that day he had seen her riding with Ralph Shamley.

Leading his horse, he walked with her up the street and met a crowd coming toward them. Sheriff Alcorte, with three deputies on either side, blocked the street.

Carse told Alcorte he intended taking Johnny to Coffin, and the Sheriff seemed relieved that he would not at this time be forced to sway him from seeking vengeance from Sam Jedrow.

At Ekert's he hired a wagon. "I'll get Ben Smiley to drive. It will be sort of crowded with you and Staggart—and Johnny. I'll ride my saddler."

"Can't Staggart drive?" Allie asked.

"I'll have to fetch Staggart," Carse said grimly. "And by this time he'll be dead drunk, if I know him."

"Then I'll drive. I can handle a wagon and team."

There was still a crowd in front of Goodfellow's. Carse left Allie in front and two men carried Johnny's body, wrapped in a tarpaulin, out to the wagon bed.

Carse asked Goodfellow where Stag had gone.

"Where he always goes at shipping time," Goodfellow said. "You'd think he'd have enough respect for his wife to stay out of Min's now, at least until her brother is buried."

Carse had tied his saddler to the tail gate. Now he drove up Chicago Street. He pulled up in front of a big two-story building with a red door. There were horses at the rack and the sound of piano music came from inside.

"This isn't a very nice place for a girl like you," Carse said, "but maybe you don't mind waiting here for a minute."

She flushed and said, "I'll wait."

When Carse opened the front door a bell jangled. A thin man with yellow hair was playing a piano. Two drunken cowboys were keeping time to the music by banging their fists on a tabletop. The yellow-haired man caught sight of Carse Boling's grim face and the music ended on a discordant note.

A tall brunette girl came out of a back room and smiled at him. He shook his head at her and said, "Where's Min?"

In a moment there were heavy footsteps from the back part of the establishment. Big Min barely managed to squeeze through the doorway that led to the parlor. When she saw Carse she lost her professional smile.

"Too bad about Johnny," she said. Then, "I guess you're after Stag." She turned to the piano player. "Lew, give him a hand."

"I can handle Stag," Carse said, and followed Min along a narrow, scented hallway. He found Stag slumped on a big brass bed, a fresh bottle of whisky in one hand. Carse jerked him to a sitting position at the edge of the bed.

"You're coming with me. We're burying Johnny tomorrow."

Staggart tried to focus his eyes. "I didn't kill him," he said drunkenly. "I didn't have nothin' to do with it."

Carse walked him through the parlor, where the yellow-haired man was again playing the piano. Two girls were sitting with the drunken cowboys.

He got Stag into the wagon seat beside Allie. Staggart pulled his hat brim low over his eyes and clung to a seat brace with both hands. From the porch Big Min said sadly, "I truly am sorry about Johnny. If it wouldn't cause talk, I'd like to be at the funeral."

"You always treated Johnny white, Min. You come. Emily will appreciate it." Carse gave her a brief wave of his hand.

After they had crossed the Missouri, Carse adjusted the stirrups on his roan and let Allie ride while he drove. Allie gave him a searching look. "Don't judge Paul until you know all the facts. Please."

The rest of the trip was made in silence. Staggart slept most of the way.

At last they saw the big log house and soon they were in the yard. Only two men were left at the ranch. Even the headquarters crew had gone to town for some helling.

Carse helped Allie to the ground. He saw that the girl was very pale. Standing in the kitchen doorway was Emily Staggart. Emily stiffened when she saw her husband drunk on the wagon seat. Her ready smile froze and she looked questioningly from Carse to Allie. Allie gave Carse a helpless look.

Carse said in a low voice, "I'll tell her."

Chapter Fourteen

EMILY WORE her beaded skirt and moccasins. She watched Staggart drop clumsily from the wagon and grip a wheel rim for support. He put a hand across his eyes as if unable to look at his wife. Then he lurched past her and entered the house.

Emily's dark gaze swung to the wagon bed. Even though the sideboards were up, she seemed to sense in Carse's grave manner the extent of her personal tragedy.

"It's Johnny," she whispered hoarsely. She came against Carse and gripped him by the arms. She peered over the tail gate. "Who killed him?"

"Sam Jedrow."

Emily closed her eyes for a moment. Then her voice lashed suddenly at Allie. "Sam Jedrow!" she cried. "And Jedrow is tied in with your brother. Why are you here?"

Allie seemed stricken. "I only came to see if I could help. I'm so sorry. . . ."

Carse said to the grief-stricken Emily, "Allie is only trying to help."

"But you told me once yourself she's painted with the same brush as her brother."

Carse waited a moment, then said, "Maybe I've changed my mind. I don't think she has any idea what's been going on."

In a moment Emily seemed to get hold of herself. "I— I'm sorry, Miss Kellerway."

When Emily went into the house, Carse said, "Go with her, Allie. She shouldn't be alone."

Johnny's body was carried into the bunkhouse. Then Carse entered the kitchen, where Allie was lighting the stove to heat coffee.

Margretha, wearing long gloves, came to the kitchen. She nodded briefly when Allie was introduced. Carse told her about Johnny.

Margretha murmured, "He was nice. A little wild, but nice." She sat down on a bench and smiled at Allie. "I'll take some coffee when it's hot," she said.

Carse said, "You might give Allie a hand."

Margretha smiled sweetly. "I'd help, dear," she told Allie, "but I have the vapors."

Then from the window Carse caught sight of Emily hurrying to the corral. She had changed her skirt for a pair of waist overalls. In her hand she carried a carbine. Carse rushed outside just as Emily was boarding the horse he had left saddled.

"Emily!" he cried. She tried to spur away but he got hold of the headstall and bore down with all his weight. The horse kicked and tried to jerk up its head. Finally he got it stopped.

He caught Emily by a wrist and pulled her from the saddle and into his arms. The carbine went flying.

"Where do you think you're going?" he demanded.

"After Sam Jedrow." She tried to squirm away, but he gripped her hard. She was small and possessed of a wiry strength. His hands locked behind her back and he pressed her against him.

"It's not a woman's place to do a thing like that," he told her.

She began to sob and then laughed wildly, and he was forced to slap the hysteria from her. The blow jolted her and she shook her head and then her eyes cleared. She leaned forward, touched her forehead briefly to his chest. "I'm all right now, Carse," she said, and he let her go. She dried her tears with the back of her hand and they walked together to the house.

The following morning there was a solemn crowd gathered in the Coffin ranchyard. The entire Coffin crew was present, and many of the townspeople. Oren Goodfellow and Si Gorman, the Radich brothers, Ralph Shamley and his wife. Sheriff Alcorte avoided Carse Boling's eyes. Big Min came out in a buggy driven by Lew, the yellow-haired piano player. She stayed apart from the others, huge in a black dress.

Emily went to her and thanked her for coming.

When Paul Kellerway rode up on a roan horse, Carse started for him, but Emily said, "Don't make a scene, Carse. Please, I've had enough." Her eyes strayed to her husband, who had sobered himself sufficiently for the ordeal of the funeral.

Kellerway came up through the crowd. He solemnly offered condolences to Emily. His black suit was powdered with dust.

Then his eyes took on a hard shine when he spotted Carse. "I understand you've been making accusations," he said. "After the funeral, if you'd care to state them to me in person, I'll be glad to accommodate you." He turned on his heel and said to Emily, "I'm stricken to learn of your brother's misfortune. I don't know who was to blame, your brother or Jedrow." Emily started to speak, but Kellerway lifted a hand and cut in: "I don't know Jedrow very well, and if I find he was lying to me— You see, I only met him recently."

Carse moved toward him. "I saw a photograph of you and Jedrow taken in Tucson. In that photo you both looked a lot younger. So it wasn't a recent picture."

Kellerway's shoulder stirred. "Well, I did meet him briefly some years ago. But I still don't know him very well."

"I wonder."

Margretha had come to the yard and overheard the conversation. "I don't think Carse should talk to you that way, Mr. Kellerway."

Kellerway gave the pale beauty an appreciative eye, and Carse could tell she enjoyed having a man look at her boldly. Especially a handsome man like Kellerway.

When the simple funeral was over, the yard emptied quickly, for this was country where there was work to be done and little time for extended sympathy.

Carse rode a quarter of a mile down the town road and waited until Big Min's buggy appeared.

"Min, I'd like to talk," he said when the buggy pulled up.

Big Min took up most of the seat. "Is it about Stag?" When Carse nodded, she said to the yellow-haired piano player, "Lew, go pick yourself a hatful of rocks."

Without a word Lew swung down and walked a short distance up the road out of earshot.

Carse said, "Min, you told me Stag talks when he gets drunk at your place. Jedrow tried to get that information out of you, didn't he?"

She was thoughtful a moment. "Is it about what happened to Johnny?"

"It's all tied in."

"I don't usually talk, Carse, but this time—" She clenched her plump hands into fists. "Well, this Jedrow come up one day and tried to pump me about Staggart.

Wanted to know if maybe his name didn't use to be Martin. And if he came here from New Mexico. He wanted to know if Stag ever mentioned once doing some killing. Jedrow must have heard Stag goes on a toot at my place every year. He offered to pay me to tell him about Stag. I told him to go to hell."

"Guess Jedrow must have convinced himself some other way that Stag was the boy he was after."

"What you think it is, Carse?" Min asked. "Has Jedrow got a knife hanging over Stag's head?"

"Looks like Stag's past has caught up with him. Thanks, Min."

Min put the tips of two fingers into her large mouth and blew a shrill blast. Lew came running. The buggy moved off toward Bellfontaine and Carse turned, surprised to see Allie Kellerway riding toward him.

He rode up and tipped his hat. Allie's brown eyes watched him a moment. Then she said bluntly, "Is Margretha anything special to you?"

"She's Stag's niece. That's it so far as I'm concerned."

Allie bit her lip. "I just wondered. When I said I was going to try to find you she gave me a terrible look."

Carse said, "Pay no attention to her." He studied Allie. The sun had faintly tanned her face. She sat her saddle like a man, legs long in the stirrups. And he suddenly knew that whatever his greedy plans might once have been concerning Margretha, he could never go through with them. A half interest in Coffin wasn't worth peddling his soul to such a woman. He leaned over the horn and said to Allie, "I've got a hunch Margretha will be gone from here soon."

They rode aimlessly, and then, in a stand of jack pine deep in an arroyo, Carse dismounted. Allie came to the ground lightly, letting the reins fall. "Do you like this country?" she asked suddenly.

He gave a short laugh as he sank to a boulder and began rolling a cigarette. "You sense my discontent."

"You're a strange man," she said. "Where did you ever get such an odd name—Carse?"

"My father named me for Kit Carson. He knew him, or claimed he did. But he thought Carson was too long. He shortened it to Carse."

"You don't talk like most of the men here. You sound educated."

He laughed bitterly. "My father sent me to school in Austin. He wanted me to be a cavalry officer. You see he could never quite believe that the South was through. He thought they would fight again and he wanted me to be ready."

She came and sank to the ground beside the boulder where he sat. She hugged her knees and watched the two horses move off to crop grass in the shade of the pines. "I suppose you wonder why I wanted to talk with you today," she said.

"Whatever the reason, I'm glad," he said candidly.

She picked up a handful of gravel, let it trickle through her fingers. "You didn't like me when we first met."

"I'd say it was the other way around. I remember the way you used to look at me."

She watched a hawk's wing cleanly cut the sky between a pine and a rock outcropping. "I'd heard some ugly stories about you and Mrs. Staggart." She looked at him in that direct way of hers. "I know now they were nothing but lies."

His face hardened. "I think I know who started those stories."

"Paul?"

"Yes."

She got to her feet and dusted her hands. "Here's what I came to tell you. I'm going to ask Paul some pointed questions. If he doesn't answer to my satisfaction, then I'm going to leave Bellfontaine." She turned and looked to the top of the arroyo, and he knew she was seeing the vast and seemingly endless broken surface of Dakota. "If Paul deserves punishment for what he has done, then I won't be here to see it."

Carse rose suddenly from the rock and stepped behind her. She turned around, startled. Then she seemed caught up with some emotion, for she stood rigid, her eyes very bright. Her lips were parted. Suddenly the weeks of tension, the bitterness that had culminated in the death of Johnny D'Orr swept aside the last barrier between himself and this girl. He knew that in the following days he would go after desperate men, and afterward he might not be alive to stand beside Allie Kellerway again. He thought of Hank Peavey, cut down before he could even taste life.

"Allie, I don't want you to leave Bellfontaine."

He put an arm across the small of her back and the strength seemed to go out of her. She sagged against his arm. Then she lifted her two hands and drew wide the collar of his shirt and pressed her lips against his throat.

"Carse," she whispered hoarsely. "From the first day we met I knew it was you. I knew that I couldn't despise you, even though I tried. And Paul sensed it." She looked up at him, the brightness more intense in her eyes. "He told me to stay away from you. Even though I reviled you, he knew." She drew back her head, biting her lips.

He picked her up and carried her into the shadows of the pines and the two horses broke apart and moved with dragging reins deeper into the arroyo to graze.

Chapter Fifteen

HE LET HER slip to the ground, where she lay looking up at him.

"I'll walk away from here, if you want," he said.

She turned on her side, placing her head on her outstretched arm. She said nothing, and in a moment he dropped beside her. He turned her so that she faced him. And suddenly her arms were about him and she held him almost fiercely. "Oh, Carse," she whispered. "I've been alone all my life. I've never, never had anything to love."

He sought her lips, straining to reach her, but she drew away from him. "Carse, one thing—"

"There's nothing to say now. Nothing." He caught her and she turned aside her head and her face was hot against his hand.

"One thing. Don't kill Paul. Don't kill him."

He drew away so he could focus his eyes upon her nearness. He saw she was flushed, her lips moist. Her eyes pleaded, but her words had started an old rancor in him. "Do you also beg for Jedrow's life?"

"Carse, you don't understand. Paul is my half brother."

"And Jedrow is what to you? Do you bargain for both of them with your body?"

She jumped to her feet. "You've turned this into something ugly."

He rose, feeling shaken and angered and somehow betrayed. "Paul Kellerway is your half brother. All right, I'll remember that. If he's guilty of having a hand in this business of Johnny D'Orr, I'll turn him over to the Sheriff. Will that satisfy you?"

"Thank you very much, Carse," she said coolly, and smoothed her hair. "Yes, it satisfies me."

He smiled fiercely. "And now?"

When he tried to kiss her she put a hand between their mouths. "You spoiled it, Carse."

"You think you can end it this way?" he demanded. "Remember, you started this thing."

"I suppose I couldn't stop you," she said. "But you would have no victory. Not this way."

98

Angrily he caught up the horses. When they were mounted she said, "I'm glad it happened this way, Carse. I'd have hated myself."

"Maybe I intended to ask you to marry me. Who knows?"

"Ask me, Carse, and I'll marry you. And take me away from this country. There are too many memories here. Johnny D'Orr, and Paul. And—and Emily Staggart."

"You still think there's something between Emily and me?" he asked. He was still angered.

Allie Kellerway shook her head. "But I'm sure she loves you."

Carse waited a long moment, then made up his mind. "When this thing is settled, I'll ask you to marry me." And suddenly he knew this was right; this was what he had been waiting for.

She regarded him gravely. "The 'thing' you speak of is Jedrow?" And when he nodded, she said, "Don't come to me with blood on your hands."

He did not reply to that. They rode slowly to Coffin, speaking of inconsequential things. Allie said she would stay a few days to help out with the housework. "Emily has enough to bear."

"Get Margretha to help you."

Allie gave him a strange smile. "She'd soil her hands. She has beautiful hands, Carse. Maybe you've noticed that she wears gloves to keep them that way."

Before they entered the yard he said, "I'm sorry about today."

"Don't be sorry. It was mutual. I wanted you as much as you wanted me. But this way is better." She smiled warmly. "Would you want a woman on your hands who had a bad conscience?"

That night in his quarters Carse considered his position. Stag had not remained sober long following Johnny's brief funeral. He kept himself locked in the bedroom most of the time.

The next morning Carse heard voices in the yard and saw Margretha and Allie about to board the rented wagon. One of the hands was on the seat to drive them to town.

Carse crossed over. During the night he had felt more relaxed than he had in months. This marriage to Allie was the right thing. But now she greeted him coolly.

Margretha smiled in that special way of hers that gave

him no warmth. "I think it best that I go with Allie to town for a few days," Margretha said. "She's offered to let me stay at her house."

Carse said, "You're Stag's kin and he needs help. You ought to stay."

Margretha turned to the wagon. She wore a gray dress and matching cloak to keep her clothing as free as possible from dust during the long ride to town. "Emily is not very good company," Margretha said sweetly, and tied a scarf over her pale hair. "I think she'll be happier if I'm gone for a few days."

"If she's short-tempered," Carse said, "you can hardly blame her. After all, her brother died tragically."

"It was a great pity," Margretha said, and pulled on long gloves so the sun would not darken her hands.

Carse drew Allie away from the wagon. The girl wore her blue shirt and jeans. "You act like I've done something wrong," he said.

Allie seemed young and fresh and clean. There was a trace of annoyance in her voice when she said, "You're not a very constant man in your affections. I think my first evaluation was correct after all."

Carse glanced at the wagon, where Margretha sat primly beside the driver. "She's been talking to you," Carse guessed.

Allie's brown eyes narrowed. "You kissed me, and made promises. And all the time you were promised to her."

"I don't intend to marry her," he said.

"She thinks you do." Allie pressed a hand against the golden hair at her temple. "I think even less of you now, for tricking her into believing you'll take her as your wife."

She skirted him and climbed into the wagon. Margretha lifted a gloved hand to Carse as the wagon started out of the yard. "Come visit me, Carse," she called.

He did not answer. In a way, he was glad that Allie and Margretha were gone. It would make his own problem simpler. He knew what must be done and for a moment when he had held Allie in his arms his resolve had weakened.

Carse got his Winchester, then stepped to the cook shack and asked Ben Smiley to fix him some jerky and cold biscuits.

The old cook looked at the rifle. "You goin' after Jedrow?"

"You figure I'd let him get away with killing Johnny?"

"Take care of yourself," Smiley said, and Carse went to one of the corrals and selected a stout dun mare. When it was saddled, Ben Smiley came out with the package of food he had prepared. Carse put the package into his saddlebag. As he swung into the saddle Emily came out of the house. She managed a wan smile as she came over to him.

"It's my fight too," she reminded him. "You should let me go with you."

"No."

"I can shoot a rifle as well as any man."

"You'd be in the way."

"Would I, Carse?" she asked softly.

They looked at each other, the tall man in the saddle and the small, shapely wife of Martin Staggart.

She brushed a hand across her eyes. "When it's over, come back to me. There's nothing at all for me if you don't." She reached up and touched his hand with the tips of her fingers. "After all, you could let the Sheriff handle it."

Carse shook his head. "Even if he would, which I doubt, it's still up to me." He looked toward the low hills with their covering of jack pine. In the distance he could see the pall of dust rising from the wagon bearing Allie and Margretha toward Bellfontaine. He felt a moment of regret when he recalled how Allie's lips had touched his throat.

Emily seemed to sense the trend of his thinking. "You liked her, didn't you?"

"Margretha?" he hedged.

"You know who I mean. The Kellerway girl."

"She'd have no faith in a man," he said. "So she wouldn't be right for me."

Without explaining, he rode out.

Chapter Sixteen

Because Ralph Shamley's Anchor spread was the nearest to Bellfontaine on the west side of the river, Carse headed that way. He arrived shortly before dark. Shamley's house was of unpainted lumber that had been ferried across the Missouri. His wife, plump and gray and calloused from the rough life she had been forced to endure, heated up supper for him.

They talked about the funeral of Johnny D'Orr, and then the talk swung to ranching.

"The day of the little outfits is about done, Carse," Shamley said glumly. It was a regular complaint of Shamley's, and Carse listened as he ate the beans and side meat Mrs. Shamley had prepared. He knew it was all too true, and he wished there were something he could do to help. The government was sending in surveyors, and there was talk of homesteading west of Bellfontaine. Shamley would be the first to feel the full effects of this invasion of the hoemen.

Carse said, "There's free land in Wyoming. A man could get a real start there with a few head of beef."

"You figure maybe to try it, Carse?"

Carse did not look up from his plate. "What makes you think I'd pull out of Coffin?"

Shamley glanced at his wife. "Well, after what happened to Johnny, and the way you and Stag been getting along, some folks are betting you'll bust up the partnership."

"So that's what they're saying." Carse broke off a chunk of bread from the loaf on the table. "You worry about Anchor. I'll take care of Coffin."

Shamley said, "I never meant to pry, Carse. But if you pull out, I know Stag won't last." He was silent a moment, then added, "The Radich brothers would like to expand. I hear they'll make Stag an offer if you leave."

"Did the Radich boys tell you to pump me when you got the chance?"

Shamley flushed. "Well, they know you and me are friends. If you hadn't come over today I was going to your

102

place and have a talk. They promised me a couple of bulls if I got the word that you figured to bust up with Stag."

Carse said, "The last I heard, the Radich boys were sore because you and some of the other small outfits were pooling to sell through Paul Kellerway." He leaned across the table and put a hand on Shamley's arm. "I don't think Wyoming would appeal to me. These winters punish a thin-blooded man like me. Guess I lived too long in Texas."

"It gets cold in Texas. I know. I was in the Army of Occupation down there after the war." Shamley broke off, embarrassed at what he had said. "I forgot, Carse, you folks was on the other side of the fence in the fight."

Carse shrugged it off. "Forget it, Ralph. The war's been over a long time. I hold no bitterness. There was plenty to regret on both sides."

When the meal was over, Carse and Shamley went into the yard for an evening smoke. One of Shamley's hands was shoeing a horse by lantern light. Carse lit a cigar he had saved from his last and tragic visit to Bellfontaine.

"Ralph, you've got your ear to the ground, and that's one of the reasons I came by here."

Shamley filled his pipe. "I figured you'd get around to it sooner or later. You're after Sam Jedrow."

"Yeah."

"It's really the Sheriff's job."

"That's what Emily says. But I feel responsible. I shouldn't have let Johnny go to Goodfellow's alone. The boys always ragged him about not drinking whisky."

"I done some of the ragging myself. I'm truly sorry. But I only done it in fun."

"I know, Ralph." Carse bit down on the cigar. "Johnny was sensitive. And men sense that. They won't let a fella alone when they spot his weakness." He turned and looked at Shamley, hunched on a log beside the house. "Where's Jedrow gone?"

Shamley knocked the dottle from his pipe and a few sparks danced across the ground and then vanished in the darkness. "Kellerway made me an offer for the beef I got to sell this year. It's the best offer I've ever had."

"In other words," Carse said, "Kellerway is buying your friendship from me."

"It ain't that, Carse," Shamley said, plainly embarrassed. "But Kellerway claims you got no right to take

Jedrow's trail. That it was a fair fight. Even Sheriff Alcorte agrees. Johnny tried to shoot Jedrow in the back."

"And Jedrow carried a gun when Alcorte set his own law that no guns were to be carried in town during shipping season."

"You got to remember this," Shamley said. "Johnny also had a gun. Alcorte says Jedrow was wrong to have that derringer up his sleeve, but so was Johnny in takin' Stag's revolver out of the money box."

Carse rose and threw down his cigar. "I don't have enough cash to top Kellerway's offer for your herd, Ralph, so I can't buy your friendship. Thanks for the meal." He started across the yard to saddle his horse.

Shamley hurried after him, stuffing his pipe into a hip pocket. "You helped me plenty, Carse, since I been here. And I ain't forgot it." He spat on the ground. "To hell with Kellerway."

Carse turned and studied the bent, shadowed figure of this rancher who had tried to make a go of a shirttail operation in the Dakotas.

"Well, Ralph?"

"Yesterday I seen Ed Lopart and Art Quince with a pack burro. They headed south along the river toward Warner Point."

"Taking supplies to Jedrow," Carse murmured.

Shamley nodded. "That's what I figured. Jedrow ain't been seen since the shooting. The boys around town figure Kellerway told him to clear out for a time."

Carse thought of the likable Art Quince and was aware of a faint regret, which he instantly put aside. "There's plenty of rough country up around Warner Point," Carse said. "It's a good place to hide out."

Shamley said, "There's at least three of them up there. Don't go alone."

"I'll manage."

Shamley rubbed the palms of his hands along his Levis. "Alcorte has put out word that he'll figure it murder if you kill Jedrow."

Carse gave a dry laugh. "Alcorte hasn't got any cows for sale. So Kellerway must have bought him off some other way."

Shamley seemed ill at ease. "Hell, Carse, I won't sell to Kellerway. I—I— Well, much as I need the money, I won't do it."

"Might be smart, Ralph. I got a hunch Kellerway is running his operation on a shoestring. Nobody ever heard of the packing house he's supposed to represent. I think he plans to option enough beef and then get the interest of one of the big packing houses. It's been done before. But you boys take the loss if the scheme fails."

Shamley thought that over, then said, "At least wait till sunup if you're bent on goin' after Jedrow."

"It's what I figured to do. A man can't do much trailing by the dark of the moon. I'll stay here if I'm welcome."

"You know better than to ask."

Carse bedded down in the bunkhouse with Shamley's three hands. It took him a long time to get to sleep. His thinking was clouded with pictures of the volatile Johnny D'Orr, of Staggart drunk and afraid of something dark from his past. And he thought of Emily, with her patient acceptance of a husband who not only was ruining her life by his cowardice, but had indirectly caused the death of her brother by knuckling down to Jedrow in the first place. And there was Margretha, the pretty vain creature who had stated her purpose coldly: to obtain part of Coffin, even if she had to marry Carse Boling to do it.

Just before he dropped off to sleep he thought of Allie. One thing he regretted above all else, that her name was Kellerway. No matter how innocent she might be in the events that had darkened this range, she still had a name that would always remind him of Johnny's death.

Carse left Anchor at dawn after eating with the Shamleys. He rode to the bluff above the river, seeing the dim outline of Merle Lanniman's ferry moored against the eastern bank. Lights still glowed across the river in Bellfontaine, and he knew the hell-raising that was part of the shipping season was still continuing.

It grew lighter. He followed the river, looking for tracks. At last he found what he sought: the tracks of two horses and a burro. He quickened his pace. It would take him a good two hours to reach Warner Point. If his assumption that Jedrow was hiding there was correct, then he would have this thing irrevocably settled before the morning was half gone. It gave him a hollow feeling in the pit of his stomach. He had counted on finding Jedrow alone. The fact that Quince and Lopart might be with him was unsettling. He wondered which way Quince would jump if it came to a showdown. As he rode he recalled that last year at shipping time he and Quince had ridden to town after roundup with Johnny D'Orr. The three of them had played poker and drunk, Johnny his Aquarius water and Carse and Quince their whisky. When Quince had gone through the money Coffin had paid him at roundup, Carse loaned the man ten dollars. He wondered if Quince remembered that. He supposed not.

Anyway, he wasn't counting on an old friendship to sway Quince.

The sun climbed and warmed his back. The palms of his hands began to perspire as the trail led inland. In any arroyo he could come upon Jedrow, who in his arrogance might not consider it important to go as far as Warner Point. He might believe himself invulnerable with the backing of Kellerway, who in turn seemed to have Sheriff Alcorte safely salted away in his hind pocket.

Under his breath he cursed the Sheriff's shortsightedness. He had always considered Alcorte fundamentally honest, even though the man was inclined to fawn over the Radich brothers for political reasons. And he couldn't blame Alcorte, in a way. Bert Radich electioneered for Alcorte and Coffin did nothing. But the fact that Alcorte had taken the word of Kellerway's friends on the shooting of Johnny D'Orr made Carse begin to wonder about the Sheriff's judgment.

The day grew warmer and he unbuttoned his shirt and then pressed a hand to his throat as he remembered the pressure of Allie's lips. Why did everything in this country turn sour on him?

A man with too much on his mind, Carse had heard once, grows careless. And, weighted with the troublesome burden of his thoughts, he did not notice the camp until he was almost upon it. His horse crested a rise, and there, not forty yards below, he saw Art Quince just hooking rawhide pack boxes on the pack saddle of a burro. Ed Lopart was drinking from a canteen, spilling water into his spiked beard.

Jedrow stood looking south. His strong hands were clasped behind his back, stocky legs widespread. He wore his yellow shirt and striped tight-fitting pants.

A roan horse that Carse took to be Jedrow's was staked

out nearby. Two other horses stood with reins dragging, grazing. A lean-to built of a tarp on a center pole was against a cut bank.

Carse heard Ed Lopart's yell of warning. He drew his rifle, levered in a shell. A snap shot tore the canteen from Lopart's hands and sent it crashing to the ground. Art Quince stood as if frozen.

Jedrow fired his revolver, and the shot, though low, set Carse's horse to pitching. He reined in the panicked animal and sent it back down the slope until he could no longer see the camp. Leaning over the horn, he saw a furrow across the animal's right foreleg where Jedrow's bullet had nicked the flesh.

Cursing himself for his own carelessness, he listened a moment, hearing Jedrow shouting at Quince and Lopart. With a lame horse, Carse knew he would be in no position to defend himself.

Cupping his hands, he shouted loudly, "Over here, boys! I think we've got 'em!"

The ruse had the desired effect. He heard Quince yell, "He ain't alone! Let's clear out!"

Carse urged his limping horse back up the rise, hoping to be able to settle the business with Jedrow, at least, in the confusion. Ed Lopart was lifting a big rifle, and Carse leveled on him with the Winchester. The man took a few staggering steps and careened into the burro, which kicked him loosely into the dirt.

Carse wasted two shots on Jedrow and Art Quince. They had caught up the two saddled horses and slashed the rope holding Jedrow's mount. With the riderless horse pounding along in their wake, they made a stand of cottonwood trees. Carse sat stiffly in the saddle as the hoofbeats of the three horses diminished. Only when he could no longer hear them did he ride down the slant and dismount. He booted his rifle and drew a revolver. Lopart lay on the ground, eyes tightly closed. The right side of his chest was stained red, and he seemed crippled in the legs, where the burro had kicked him.

Keeping an eye on the cottonwoods, Carse knelt down beside the man. Lopart opened his eyes. He did not look so hard now. Now that he had time to study him closely, Carse could see that the spike beard had been grown to cover a badly receding chin.

Carse drew the man's belt gun and threw it into the

brush. Then he pulled a Sharps rifle from beneath Lopart. "So you use a Sharps," Carse said.

"For special work," Lopart managed to say. "Hit a man with that and he don't get up."

"The main thing is to get him," Carse said, and pushed the rifle out of Lopart's reach. "The first time you tried for me, you missed."

"The sun was in my eyes," Lopart said, gritting his teeth at the pain of his chest wound.

"And you killed a kid by mistake."

"You moved just at the second I squeezed the trigger." Carse put the revolver muzzle against Lopart's temple. "I ought to blow out your brains. Hank Peavey was a good boy. And he died because the sun got in your eyes."

"Better it was you that died?" Lopart asked thinly.

"Who told you to try to kill me?" Carse demanded.

"Go to hell."

"Kellerway won't pay the bills where you're going."

"Who said it was Kellerway?"

"A guess, but a good one, Lopart." Carse holstered his revolver. "You're going to town with me. You'll tell the Sheriff you killed Hank Peavey." He rose to get a canteen and give Lopart a drink. When he returned, Lopart was dead.

Carse's horse was in no condition for the hard riding necessary to overtake Jedrow and Quince. He loaded Lopart's body on the burro and made the long ride to Bellfontaine.

He blamed himself for Jedrow's escape. Had he not been daydreaming, he would not have ridden so close to their camp. But it was too late now for recriminations. At least he had avenged one death. But it gave him no satisfaction that this day he had been forced to kill a man.

Chapter Seventeen

WHEN CARSE appeared in town with Lopart's body, he created quite a stir. Word spread quickly and by the time he pulled up in front of Sheriff Alcorte's neat stone jail a large crowd had gathered.

Hearing the commotion, Alcorte came out, thumbs hooked in wide galluses. When he saw Lopart's body being cut from the burro he turned angrily on Carse.

"I warned you!" he cried. "I warned you not to go after them!"

Carse turned on him. He told how he had come upon the camp unexpectedly and how Quince and Jedrow had got away. "Lopart killed Hank Peavey. He admitted it in so many words."

"How do I know you're telling the truth?" the Sheriff demanded.

"You'll have to take my word for it, Luke. It's a certainty Lopart won't tell you different."

Alcorte jerked on his galluses a few times in anger, then told two of the men in the crowd to carry Lopart down to the shanty in back of Apperson's feed store that was used as an undertaking establishment.

Then he jerked his head at Carse. "Let's talk," he said gruffly, and led the way into the jail office.

Alcorte shut the street door and the one leading to the two cells behind the office. He sank to a swivel chair under a gun cabinet.

"Carse, I'm in the middle in this thing," the Sheriff said. "You think I'm picking on you, but I'm only the sheriff. I got elected to office and I'm trying to run it fairly."

"Kellerway hired Lopart to kill me. Lopart killed Hank Peavey by mistake instead of me."

"But you can't prove it, Carse," Alcorte snapped. "I don't know anything about Kellerway, but he seems honest enough. I can't hold him responsible for hiring Lopart or Jedrow. Kellerway is repping for a big Chi packing house. Shamley and some of the other small operators are going to get a good price for their beef from him."

109

"They haven't seen any money yet."

"Well, I'm sure they will." Alcorte got to his feet and paced the office. "Now about the shooting of Johnny D'Orr."

"Why discuss it?" Carse said angrily. "You've already made up your mind who was to blame."

The Sheriff's face reddened. "I wasn't in Goodfellow's when Johnny got shot. When I got there nobody seemed to know exactly what had happened. Johnny was dead with a forty-five in his hand. Jedrow had a derringer. I started to light into Jedrow when Stag spoke up. Stag said it was Johnny's fault. That Jedrow only defended himself." The Sheriff shrugged helplessly. "What could I do, Carse, when you came busting in and claimed Jedrow murdered Johnny? You didn't even see the shooting. I had to take the word of those that had. And if Staggart, Johnny's brother-in-law, thought Jedrow was in the right, I don't see what else I could do."

Carse looked grim. "I can't understand Stag's turning against Johnny that way. Not at a time like that."

"But maybe he didn't. Maybe Stag told it right—that Johnny tried to kill Jedrow." Alcorte passed over a cigar. Carse took one and they fired up. "If Stag lied about how it happened," Alcorte went on, "he must have a reason."

"I imagine he has, or thinks he has," Carse muttered.

"One thing I want understood, Carse. Our talk today don't alter how I regard the idea of your settling with Jedrow on your own. You'd better not try bringing him in like you did Lopart."

Carse said, "I understand from Ralph Shamley that the Radich boys are interested in buying Coffin."

"That's no news," Alcorte said. "Bert told me that over a year ago." Something in Carse's eyes made the Sheriff add hastily, "Now don't you go tryin' to tie Johnny and the rest that's happened in with Bert and Ardo."

Carse went out and closed the door. He took the burro to Ekert's and had the stableman doctor the bullet nick on his horse's foreleg. Then he hired a mount, changed saddles, and rode to Goodfellow's. Just as he dismounted he saw Allie coming along the walk.

She greeted him coolly. Today she wore a starched shirt-waist and a black pleated skirt. Her hair was pinned up and she looked too dignified to be the girl he remembered that day in the arroyo.

"I see you've started with your gun," she said, her brown eyes watching his face severely.

"You mean Lopart?" He looped reins over the rail.

"You've killed once. Now I suppose the next time will be easier."

"I've killed before," he said with a trace of anger, "to keep from being killed. I didn't like it. I don't like what happened today. Or maybe you'd rather have seen Lopart pack me in today on the burro."

Her face lost color. "I didn't mean that, Carse."

He started away, wondering how this could be the same woman he had held that day. She caught up with him.

She said, "I just don't want you to keep on killing."

"Afraid it might be your brother next?"

"Yes, I am," she said, and they halted on the walk.

"Have you had your grand talk with him?" he asked, his voice edged with sarcasm. "You were going to ask him point-blank about his objectives in this country. If they didn't meet with your approval, you were going to leave Bellfontaine. Remember?"

She bit her lip. "Under the circumstances I could see no reason for asking Paul. Things have changed between you and me." She looked away and her voice was shaky as she said: "After all, we can hardly mean anything to each other now."

Passers-by skirted them on the walk. There was a constant flow of men in and out of the Red Devil. The brassy music was still brassy; a drunk hooted.

Suddenly the words tumbled from him. "Why did you believe Margretha? I don't know what she said, but it was obviously a lie."

If Allie's face had been wistful a moment before, it changed suddenly. "She's a sweet girl, Carse—despite her possible faults. She has no friends here except you and of course her uncle. I—I think you will marry her."

"Because she's Staggart's niece I should put a ring on her finger?"

"You wished to gain a fifty-per-cent interest in Coffin," Allie went on grimly. "Oh, I heard all about it. And you intend to marry her to gain that end. And you made sure she would *have* to marry you." Allie's brown eyes were bright. "Do I make myself clear?"

"I'm not hearing well today. Maybe you can clarify that last statement."

Allie's face was red. "The day she arrived here, Carse. The day you drove her to Coffin. On the way you—you took advantage of her."

It was Carse's turn to redden.

"The guilt's on your face, Carse," Allie said.

"She's a lying little—"

"She's been to see Dr. Bishop. She told me so herself. No woman would lie about a thing like that." Allie turned from him and walked rapidly across the street to her brother's office. As she reached the stairs she started running.

In Goodfellow's the talk was of the shooting of Ed Lopart. Carse didn't want to discuss it with the men who crowded about him, and they seemed to resent it. He had a drink and then another.

Bert and Ardo Radich entered and said they'd like a word with Carse. Carse followed them to a table.

Bert Radich combed fingers through his curly beard and gave Carse a friendly smile. "How much you want for your interest in Coffin?"

"Not for sale."

Bert Radich's eyes hardened. "I could convince you otherwise."

"And Bert can," Ardo Radich said. "He sure can."

Carse ignored the pale younger Radich brother. "Bert, you can't bluff me."

"Carse, I'll put it to you straight. If Kellerway keeps up the pressure on you and Stag and forces you to bust up, then I'm going to bid in on Coffin. I've got nothin' against you or Stag. But we're big now and we're goin' to be bigger. If we get Coffin, then we'll be the biggest outfit in the territory."

"Why the ambition all of a sudden?"

"The government's talking about homesteaders, and me and Ardo don't like that. You know and I know the bigger an outfit is, the more political power it has."

"You've proved that in this county," Carse said thinly.

"If you mean Alcorte, you're right. He's an honest sheriff. A crooked one plays both sides, and we don't want that."

"You elect Alcorte so he plays your side of it."

Bert Radich smiled. "At election time Forty-four gets behind our candidate. We send all our riders out to talk up Alcorte and make sure of votes. What did Coffin ever do to elect a sheriff? Not one damn thing. So when the chips start falling, Alcorte naturally sees that more of 'em fall on our side than on Coffin's."

"You're not telling me a thing I don't already know," Carse snapped.

"The main thing I'm telling you is this: Me and Ardo see a chance to expand. We're not going to pass it up."

"And you'll stomp your friends to do it."

"It's business, Carse." Bert Radich leveled a heavy forefinger. "Now here's what I want to tell you." He lowered his voice so that it was barely audible above the noisy clamor of the barroom. "You fight your fight alone, understand? Don't take the Coffin crew and try to wipe out Kellerway's bunch. You could do it, all right. But we'd have a range war on our hands. I don't want that."

"You're threatening me, Bert."

"Take it any way you like. But remember this: You ride after Kellerway with the Coffin crew behind you and I'll saddle up my Forty-four boys. It'll be one hell of a fight, and a lot of boys will get buried where they fall."

"I might call your bluff."

"Yeah, you might. But the blood that's spilled will be on your hands."

Carse stiffened in his chair. "We've been neighbors for a long time, Bert. I didn't think that when the going got rough my neighbor would put his hand in my pocket."

Bert Radich shrugged. "What the hell, you'd do the same. You've got to expand today to make anything. So if you and Stag split up, I'll be there with an offer to buy you out. And if Kellerway's hole card ain't as good as he seems to think and you and Stag whip him, then we'll still be neighbors. Now have a drink, Carse."

"Keep your whisky—neighbor," Carse said, and went outside.

He rode slowly along Chicago Street. As he passed Big Min's he thought: Stag gets rid of the pressure this way. Why not me?

But he passed on and soon was crossing the Missouri on the ferry.

A black cloud of despair engulfed him all the way to Coffin. When he rode into the ranchyard he found Emily just coming down the slope from her brother's grave. He waited for her. When she saw him she gave a glad cry and ran to meet him.

"You're all right," she said. "You didn't find Jedrow. Oh, Carse, I was so worried!"

He told her about jumping the camp and how Jedrow had got away. He didn't tell her about Lopart. She'd learn about that soon enough.

They walked together behind the barn and along the corrals. Emily chewed a piece of straw. He could see the straight part in her black hair.

"Stag still hasn't come out of it?" he asked.

"He's got a bottle with him night and day. He's locked himself up in the bedroom." She removed the straw from her mouth, looked at the marks her small teeth had made in it. She rubbed her shoulders and shivered. And he felt it too. A chill in the air. Winter was coming.

Somehow he could not bear the thought of snow piled deep about the house, the blizzards, the riding in storms, wet clothing, freezing hands. He thought of the dull gray sky, the time when men's tempers grew shorter than the short dark days.

Suddenly it struck him that there was no need to go through another winter like that, and he wondered why he had not considered it before. "Em, we've no longer got anything at Coffin."

"I've got nothing," Emily said dispiritedly. "But you have Margretha."

"You know what she is, and so do I. She's spread a story about me that I don't like."

"I know. I called her a liar to her face."

"Thanks, Em. I'm glad you had faith enough in me."

Emily studied his face. "Allie heard the story and she believed it?"

"Yeah, she believed it."

They started walking again, and Carse said, "I have nothing left in this country. You had Johnny, and now he's gone."

Emily clenched her fists. "I have a husband."

"You've kept your part of the bargain, Em. He's failed you. You owe him nothing."

Emily groped for his hand, her face averted so he could not see her eyes. "Could we do it, Carse? Could we go away somewhere and start again?"

"We could, Em."

"Could we look at ourselves in a mirror and not turn away?"

He said gruffly, "Don't talk to me about a woman's conscience. I've already heard that one." He was thinking of that day with Allie in the arroyo. Emily looked at him with some surprise.

"It's not my conscience," she said. "I'd just want to feel that I was doing the right thing. For Stag."

"How can you even consider him, after all he's done?"

"But he's my husband. I made a vow when I married him."

"Vows are made to be broken, Em," he said bitterly, and flung out a hand toward the far reaches of the sky. "These are changing times. Maybe once vows meant something. But not now. The world's gone crazy, Em. The Civil War changed everything. Things will never be the same." The bitterness deepened in his voice as she watched him with an odd look in her eyes. "I was seven years old when the war started. It was a vicious, bloody thing."

"Are you trying to tell me that because of a war there's no meaning left to life? No decency? No honesty?"

"Em, you're the only decent thing left on this earth."

"You're a bitter man, Carse. I never knew how bitter."

He caught her by the waist and swung her lightly to the top rail of the corral. "Em, leave Stag. Come with me to Texas. We'll take my twenty per cent of the herd. Leave Stag with his bottle and his cowardice."

She stood for a moment, her dark head tilted back as she peered to the west, where the first red banners of clouds marked the closing of the day. "Perhaps I'm more Indian than you think, Carse. I don't know. My mother's people have a different moral code. The man can do what may please him and it's not the woman's place to question." She gave a small shrug. "I know all about Stag, and what he does in town every year after shipping."

"But you're half French-Canadian. You're not an Indian. Not where morals are concerned. Stag's been rotten to you."

She said gravely, "Do you really want me, Carse?"

He peered up at her sitting so small on the corral fence, her back straight, hands folded in her lap. In the moment it took him to answer he instinctively touched his throat at the spot where Allison Kellerway had kissed him that day. Then resolutely he pushed the memory aside. "I want you, Em," he said, and held out his arms. She dropped from the fence into his embrace.

Then they walked together to the house. From the kitchen they saw that Staggart had come out of the bedroom. He lay on the sofa, apparently in a stupor.

Carse said, "Get some of your things together. You won't need much. We'll travel light and fast." He took a deep breath. "I'll tell Stag what we intend to do."

Before she could protest or warn him to be careful, he went into the front room. Stag roused himself and looked at him out of bloodshot eyes. He looked as if he had aged ten years in the past few weeks.

Carse felt revolted at sight of this wreck of a man. He shook Stag's shoulder. "You don't deserve a wife," he said harshly. "Em and I are going away."

But Staggart appeared not to comprehend. He settled back against the sofa and closed his eyes. He began to snore. In a moment Emily came to look down at her husband. She carried a small bundle of her clothing.

Carse said, "I told him, but I doubt if he ever heard me. The drunken pig."

Emily went to the kitchen and in a moment returned with a fresh bottle of whisky. She pulled the cork with her small white teeth and put the bottle beside the sofa. "He'll need a drink when he wakes up," she said.

"My God, even when he's treated you like a dog you still look after him."

Emily clutched the bundle of clothing to her bosom. "He'll have nobody to look after him now." Then she moved briskly to the back door and into the yard.

Carse saddled two horses and tried not to look at her. He could see that she had been weeping.

They rode swiftly. He had not wanted to say good-by to any of the hands. It would be like turning a knife blade in his stomach. He didn't want to see old Ben Smiley looking at him and to know what the old cook was thinking: Carse, you're running off with another man's wife.

"I'll pick up a crew in Bellfontaine," Carse said. "It's best we start with a new bunch. The less they know about us, the better. I've got some money in the bank. We'll buy a wagon and supplies. We'll take nothing from Coffin but my share of the beef."

"I'm glad you want it this way, Carse. I don't want anything from Stag. Nothing. Otherwise I couldn't let myself do this."

Chapter Eighteen

THEY RODE toward Bellfontaine, and the darkness thickened. He would get his crew in town, then swing south and west. He knew where some of the best Coffin beef was scattered. They would work the south end of the range, far from headquarters. He would take 2,500 head of beef. It was not as much as he had coming, but then, he was taking enough from Stag. He was taking his wife.

Emily suddenly pulled up when it got full dark. "Let's camp here." There was a note of desperation in her voice.

Carse said, "We can make Bellfontaine tonight. We'll just follow the road."

"No. I want to stop here." Her voice shook. She hugged herself against the night chill. "Carse, build a fire."

There was a new awkwardness between them. Before their friendship had been a fine thing. The touching of hands, the smiles. He built the fire and staked the horses. He was glad it was dark, because he was certain he blushed when he spread the blankets. He turned his back to her and sat upon the ground and smoked a cigarette.

"Carse," she called to him presently.

He felt a tightening in his throat. A different, new feeling. Guilt, perhaps, he told himself. He turned to where she lay in the blankets, her small face white in the glow of the campfire. He knelt down beside her.

"Emily." His voice was choked.

She closed her eyes.

He said, "Why did it have to be tonight? We've plenty of time. You're still worked up over Johnny. Over the way Stag's been acting."

A small hand came out of the blankets and gripped his. "Don't talk about it, Carse."

They were in a clearing surrounded by jack pine. Firelight washed over the high branches. In the distance he thought he heard the screech of a lynx.

"I don't want you to think I'm going away with you for—for only one reason." He fumbled, embarrassed. "I want to help you, Em."

117

She shut her eyes again, and he could see the muscles along her small jaws and she clenched her teeth. "I want you, Carse—tonight, now. I want to close the door forever on my past. If I'm going to do this thing, it's the way it's got to be." She opened her eyes and stared at him. "You understand, Carse?"

"I understand." The wind stirred the campfire, sent sparks whirling into the black maw of the sky.

"I've got to plunge into this, Carse. Blindly, without thought. Then it will be over. Because you understand that afterward I could never go back to Stag. Never."

He leaned over and pressed his mouth against hers. In a moment he drew back. He smiled and said, "It's no good, is it, Em?"

She began to weep softly.

He looked across the campfire to the saddles on the ground, his gun rig draped from one of the horns. "I'll saddle up," he said.

Emily said, "I wanted to, Carse. I really wanted to, but—"

"You taught me something tonight, Em," he said softly. "You're bound to certain people in this life. Right or wrong, you're bound to them. Stag is my partner. We built Coffin together. Yet when he's afraid of something I turn my back."

The horses nickered. Carse stiffened and put a hand to his thigh. He cursed himself for leaving his gun with the saddles.

Jedrow's voice angled in from the shadows of the trees. "Been layin' for you, Boling. Been hanging around the ranch. And now I follow you two and find *this*."

Jedrow's voice came from beyond the fire. And because of the leaping flames, Carse was blinded to any move the big man might make. He felt a worm of fear begin to uncoil within him. He looked down at Emily Staggart. She had pulled the blankets up under her chin. Her dark eyes were afraid.

"Carse," she whispered, "don't let him touch me."

Jedrow must have heard her, for he had come out of the trees to stand at the edge of the clearing, holding a rifle. "Mrs. Staggart, I don't aim to harm you," he called.

"That day at the house," Emily cried. "You tried to get me alone."

"No. You didn't understand, Mrs. Staggart. I tried to tell you."

Emily whispered to Carse, "My gun. In my pocket."

Carse, still on his knees, put out a hand to the small pile of Emily's clothing. In the pocket of her Levis he felt the bulge of a small revolver.

Emily said loudly to cover Carse's movements, "Because you were angered at me you killed my brother!"

Jedrow moved a step nearer the fire. "It just happened that way. I was waiting for Boling that day in town. If he'd come into Goodfellow's, it would have been him instead of your brother. I'm damn sorry it was that way, Mrs. Staggart. But your brother was a troublemaker. And we figured he'd have to be got rid of. I wanted to tell you that day at the ranch to send him away."

Carse drew the gun from the pocket of Emily's discarded Levis. It was a small pearl-handled weapon.

Then Art Quince's voice angled in from the deeper shadows. "By God, Carse, I heard them stories about you and Emily Staggart but I never believed 'em. Not till we caught you two in the blankets." Quince sounded drunk.

Carse said, "Your eyesight's bad, Art. Emily's got a sprain. She fell from her horse. Come closer and take a look if you don't believe me."

"Stay away from him," Jedrow ordered from across the clearing.

Carse forced a scornful laugh. "Art, how much are you getting out of this? A piece of this two-bit cattle empire they figure on launching here?"

Jedrow said, "You come with us, Boling. Just step over here where I can watch you good."

Emily whispered, "Please, Carse, don't leave me alone with them."

"Don't worry." He licked his dry lips and got to his feet. "I tell you, Mrs. Staggart is bad hurt. I've got to get her to town to a doctor."

Jedrow said, "I know how bad hurt she is, all right. Don't try to fool me. Like I said, I been following you. Now you come over here. When we're gone Mrs. Staggart can clear out." Jedrow added, "And nobody will ever know what we seen here tonight. That right, Art?"

"Sure, Sam."

"You're damn right it better be sure," Jedrow shouted at Quince across the campfire. "You ever talk about this and you'll be sorry it's me after you. You'll wish it was an Oglala runnin' his war lance through you from crotch to head."

Emily whispered hoarsely, "Carse, don't go with them. They intend to kill you."

Carse said loudly, "All right, Jedrow. I'm coming." He had gauged Art Quince's position from the sound of the man's voice in the darkness. Now he moved that way, skirting the fire. From a corner of his eye he got his first glimpse of Quince. But he continued walking slowly toward Jedrow, who stood at the far end of the clearing holding a rifle.

Carse halted when he was abreast of Quince. "Art, I'm sorry you had to get mixed up with a bunch like this."

Quince said lamely, "A fella's got to make a dollar the best way he can."

"I offered you a job."

"But, Carse, they'll pay big. A bonus. Enough for me to get a stake. You done right well, Carse. You're only a few years older than me, but you own part of a ranch. Me, I got nothin'. It's gettin' late. I just want a start, Carse. Nothin' more."

"So you're going to take me into the dark and shoot me. Is that your idea of a start?"

He moved a step closer so he could see Quince's face in the reflection of the fire. The man held a carbine. At his belt was a revolver.

From the opposite end of the clearing Jedrow said, "That's enough talk. Bring him over here, Quince. And be careful. He's tricky."

Carse forced a scornful laugh. "Art, you owe me ten dollars from last year."

Art Quince said, "I ain't forgotten. I'll pay."

"You won't have to pay. You're going to take an old friend out and shoot him. Art, you've fallen pretty low."

Quince had moved up closer and Carse suddenly fired Emily's revolver at Jedrow. Jedrow cursed and threw a wild shot with his rifle. Quince, caught flat-footed, tried to shift his carbine so as to cover Carse. Carse shot him, and as Quince fell, Carse got behind him. He jerked free Quince's belt gun. Two of Jedrow's shots hit Quince. Quince was already falling and the heavy slugs turned him around so that he struck the ground on his back.

Dropping to one knee, Carse emptied the revolver he

had snatched from Art Quince's holster. He could no longer see Jedrow, but he could hear the big man lumbering off through the trees. Jedrow was cursing wildly. In a moment there was the racket of hoofbeats. There was another shot from Jedrow's rifle, a lance of orange flame in the shadows. Carse heard the bullet strike the trunk of a tree behind him. Quickly he ran to the fire and kicked dirt on it as the hoofbeats of Jedrow's horse died. Then in the darkness he ran to Emily.

"It's all right, Em," he said, and held her trembling body against him. They both listened then and there was only the faint sound of Jedrow's horse in the distance. "He's gone, Em. I think I hit him."

"He frightens me so," Emily said, and dug her fingers into his shoulder. "What about Quince?"

"I'll have a look. You get dressed."

He crossed the clearing to where Jedrow had stood. He struck a match and saw in the flickering glow a fresh trail of blood leading off into the trees. Then he moved to where Quince had fallen. He risked another match and stared down into Quince's white face. One of Jedrow's bullets had caught him high on the forehead. Carse felt sick at his stomach. He got some brush and rocks and covered the body as best he could. He found Art's horse and unsaddled it and turned it loose.

Then he crossed to where Emily, fully dressed, was rolling up the blankets. "I'll get word to Alcorte about Quince," Carse said.

"I suppose you must." Emily sighed. "Then everyone will know we were here together."

"Quince can't talk and I don't think Jedrow will. Funny, but I'd swear Jedrow's in love with you."

"Oh, God, what a thought!" Emily groaned.

Carse gripped her arm. "Shall we go home, Em?"

"Yes. Let's go home."

Chapter Nineteen

THEY RODE HOME silently. In the parlor they found Staggart sitting up on the sofa, the bottle between his booted feet. Emily laid her bundle of clothing on the table.

Staggart looked from Carse to Emily, then said, "It took me a while to get it through my head what you said, Carse. But I finally did." Stag got unsteadily to his feet. "You son-of-a-bitch, you stole my wife!"

Emily started forward but Carse blocked her with an outflung arm. "Emily and I tried to run away. It didn't work. She's your wife and she couldn't forget that, no matter how you've treated her. And I want you to understand this, Stag: Emily is coming back to you exactly as she left. You understand that? She's the same woman. Nothing's happened to change her."

Staggart looked at him dully a moment.

Carse said, "I'm your partner. I was going to run away, but now I'm back. We're both back. And now, by God, you're going to tell me what hold Kellerway and Jedrow have over you!" Carse rolled up his shirt sleeves. "You'll tell me now or I'll beat the hell out of you until you do tell."

Some semblance of sanity seemed to return to Staggart's eyes. He turned to his wife. "Em, is it true what he said? You and him—I mean, you're still my wife?"

"I couldn't love him, Stag." She stood small and dark, her fingers working. "For years I thought I might be in love with Carse. But it was only a thought, nothing more. He would smile at me and I would feel good for the whole day. He was always doing nice things for me." She gazed into her husband's face. "I don't know what love is, Stag. It isn't what I tried to feel for Carse tonight. Maybe it isn't what I feel for you. But I'm your wife. I married you. I can't turn away when you need me. I'll never turn away unless you ask me."

She came to the big drunken man and took one of his rough hands. "Tell us, Stag. Don't hide from it any longer. Why are you afraid?"

122

Staggart suddenly sank to the sofa and buried his head in his folded arms. He sobbed. And Carse, feeling ashamed to see this man in his degredation, started to go.

Emily said firmly, "Stay, Carse. It's got to be settled tonight."

After a few moments Staggart lifted his head. His eyes were almost swollen shut from his weeping. "Go ahead," he snarled at Carse. "Laugh. You know I'm yellow! I could have kicked Jedrow off the place, but I was scared. My brother-in-law is murdered and I'm afraid. My best friend tries to run off with my wife. And then they both come and tell me they couldn't do it. That they owe something to me. And I cry. I cry like a goddamn woman!" He lunged to his feet, hands clenched. "Like a goddamn woman. Me, Staggart!" He swayed. "Carse, you ever see me afraid of anything before Jedrow came here?"

"No."

"Em, you asked me in so many words why I went to Min's. Why I got drunk. I did it to keep from going crazy. Because I was scared. I knew one day somebody would walk out of that other life I had. And they did. I was sittin' in Goodfellow's one afternoon playing cards. And I seen Sam Jedrow. I wanted to die right then. I wanted to die, Em."

He quieted then and stood with his chin on his breastbone. Emily pushed him back gently until the sofa caught him and he slumped down. She handed him the bottle. "Take a drink. A good long drink. Then tell us."

Stag took a pull at the bottle, wiped his mouth with the back of a hand. He seemed to have regained control of himself. "Eleven years ago a fella named Elmo Hoyt and me ran some cows back in the Mogollons in New Mexico. It was rough going and we had losses because the 'Paches gave us plenty of trouble. We had a shack built and Elmo had himself a Mexican girl named Luz. One day Elmo, who was always trying to find some color, thought he stumbled on a silver strike. Elmo took some ore samples to the assayer in Silver City and done some bragging. The more he got to thinking about it, the more he figured if he did have a strike there was no use in sharing it. He come back from Silver City drunk."

Staggart closed his eyes and took another drink. "Elmo told this Mex girl, Luz, what he aimed to do. He was going to lay for me. But when I come in the shack Luz grabbed his gun, yelling for me to run." Staggart shuddered. "God, I can still hear her screaming. Elmo's gun went off and she got shot through the heart. And before Elmo could line on me again, I killed him."

"Where do Kellerway and Jedrow fit into this?" Carse asked.

"Kellerway was hanging around the assay office in Silver City in them days, trying to get a line on anybody who'd made a strike. He passed himself off as a mining engineer. Well, he was one of them Elmo had bragged to. So Kellerway comes ridin' out to the shack to see Elmo and finds him and the girl dead. I tell you I was near crazy. I didn't know what to do." He gave Carse a long look. "You see, killin' a man is one thing. But finding a dead woman is something else. I had gone out to dig a grave, and while I was gone Kellerway come and seen the bodies. He puts a gun on me, and says if I'll sign over the property where Elmo had made his strike he'll give me a chance to ride for it."

"And you didn't do it."

"I told him to go to hell," Staggart went on. "It was a mistake. He come back with a posse. Jedrow was a deputy then and he held off the crowd and got me to jail. The trial was that afternoon and I was supposed to hang at sunrise. I tell you the town was riled. They claimed I killed Luz and Elmo and they'd have hung me twice if they could. Well, I managed to get away. I headed south and zigzagged to throw off anybody tryin' to find my trail. I come to Dakota and got my start."

Emily sat down on the sofa beside her husband. "Stag, why didn't you tell me?"

"You don't understand," Stag said fiercely. "I couldn't take a chance on you turnin' against me, Em. You see, there's plenty in this country who have killed a man. But it puts a brand on you if folks think you'd murder a woman in cold blood."

Carse shoved his hands deep in his pockets. He was tired and unnerved from what the past weeks had brought him. "You could have told me, Stag. I'd understand something like that."

Stag studied the pattern of one of the Indian rugs on the floor. "I would have, Carse. But when Jedrow showed up here I began hearing stories about you and Em. I wanted to trust you, but—"

"Then you thought if I married your niece it would keep me away from Emily. And with a fifty-per-cent interest you figured I'd be sure to stand behind you." Carse gave a weary shake of his head. "You should know you wouldn't have to buy me."

Emily's eyes were bright. "They've been clever all through this thing. Spreading lies, making Stag suspicious, and at the same time holding the threat of the noose over his head."

Stag seemed spent. "I'm glad it's over. I'm glad I got it off my chest."

"Kellerway made you pay him off," Carse guessed, "by turning over the herd we figured to ship. Right?"

"Yeah. But he wouldn't stop there."

"His kind never does."

"I can see now that he planned to get rid of Johnny. Then you, Carse. Then me."

"I already told you that," Carse reminded him.

"I know, but I couldn't think straight then." Staggart groped for Emily's hand. "Em would have been the only one left, and he thought he could pressure her into selling out cheap. At least, that's the way I got it figured."

Emily squared her shoulders. "He couldn't have got rid of me that easy."

Stag searched his wife's determined, pretty face. "You've got more fight in you than I have."

Emily got to her feet. "We could tell Sheriff Alcorte the story and get his advice."

Stag's face went gray. "You don't understand. I been tried and convicted of killin' a man and a woman. I been sentenced to hang. All they got to do is to take me back to New Mexico and put my neck in a rope."

"A new trial would clear you," Carse said.

Stag gave a vigorous shake of his head. "There wouldn't be a new trial. There's plenty of people left there who remember what happened. Luz was only a dance-hall girl, but when she was dead you'd have thought she was the most saintly woman that ever drew breath." A shudder racked his body. "I tell you, I know what I'm talkin' about. Once they know for sure where I am, they'll take me back to New Mexico and hang me the day I get there." He lurched to his feet. "I tell you I got an unholy fear of hangin'. Once when I was a kid I saw a fella strung up. It was terrible. I never forgot it."

Carse said grimly, "We've got two choices. Either we talk to the Sheriff or we take care of Paul Kellerway."

Emily was quick to veto this. "Killing him won't clear Stag. It's got to be done right. We've got money enough to hire a good lawyer. We can fight this thing, Stag."

"Em, you don't understand. I couldn't face this country if the story got out."

"But you say you didn't kill the woman, and that you only shot your partner in self-defense."

"But nobody will believe me, Em. It's in the court record. I was found guilty of murdering Luz and Elmo, so I could get hold of the silver claim."

"Stag, the only ammunition people like Kellerway have is fear," Emily said. "If you're not afraid of them they can't touch you."

"But they can. Even if Kellerway and Jedrow are killed, there's still the law in New Mexico. The way they look at it down there, I'm eleven years overdue for a hanging. They won't waste time on me."

They talked it out for another hour and at last Staggart wearily agreed to go along with them and let Sheriff Luke Alcorte handle the matter.

"Alcorte has let Kellerway charm him," Emily said. "But once he knows the truth about the man, he'll be forced to act."

Carse started to tell Emily and Stag what he knew about the Radich brothers' plans to pounce on Coffin if they saw an opportunity. But he decided it would only complicate the issue further.

"And what if Alcorte doesn't see things your way?" Carse asked Emily.

"Then Stag and I will go to Canada to live. They'll never find us there. I'll give up everything here, if necessary. But Stag has got to be cleared."

Chapter Twenty

THERE WAS a brief rumble of thunder over Bellfontaine when Paul Kellerway carried out his sister's portmanteau to the buggy he had rented to take her to the train. The driver from Ekert's waited in the seat.

Kellerway gave Allie his practiced smile. "Believe me, this is the right thing to do. You own an interest in the company I'm forming and—"

"Just so I'm repaid the two thousand dollars I loaned you," she said tartly. "That's all I want."

A shadow crossed his yellow-brown eyes. "There's no crime in taking a little profit, is there?"

"Dad didn't want you to have any of that money. I realize it now. That's why he left it and the acreage in Arizona to me. But I guess you've always had your own way, so you knew you could talk me out of the money. And you did." She looked at the lean, handsome face framed by the graying hair at the temples. "No, I don't want any profit. Save that for yourself and your Mr. Jedrow."

Her tone caused his shoulders to stiffen under his black coat. As usual, he looked immaculate. "Jedrow's a good man," he said thinly. "A better man than your Carse Boling."

She picked up a wicker valise and started for the door.

Kellerway said maliciously, "I know why you're leaving. It isn't because of the business methods you claim to disapprove of. You're leaving because of Carse Boling."

Her face flamed. "My private life is none of your business!"

"Still the same old temper," he observed, and tried hard to keep irritation from showing in his voice. It rankled that she had smugly reminded him of the money he had borrowed. And to want no return on her investment was a further insult.

"Don't bother to come to the station with me," she said shortly.

"I didn't intend to, Allie," he said, his voice softening a little. "I have a business appointment." After all, he told himself, she had acreage in Arizona left to her alone by their father. It might be expedient to part on friendly terms. A man could not always gauge his fortunes. Something unforeseen could happen here and he might wish her to mortgage the property one day so as to give him a start somewhere else. And he was fully confident that he could charm her into anything, once he put his mind to it.

"Allie, I'm sorry things didn't work out for you here," he said, catching her at the door. "I can understand how you feel about Boling. He should have told you he planned to marry Margretha Lenrick."

Allie said, "You seem pretty fond of her yourself."

He was taken by surprise.

"Or is my eyesight bad?" she persisted. "I could have sworn I saw you dining with her at the hotel last night."

"It was business," Kellerway said easily. "After all, she's Staggart's only kin. If Staggart takes me in as a partner, it's good business to make sure I'm on the right side of his niece. Especially if she marries Carse Boling. I don't think he likes me very well. If she puts in a good word for me, it'll help all around in my transactions with Coffin."

"You're such a liar," Allie said, and went out to the buggy.

Because cattle were still being shipped, her accommodations on the train east were not of the best. The single passenger coach was coupled to the engine, and cattle cars were strung out behind. The day was sultry and the odor of cattle appalling. Thunderheads had built up in the northern sky and she noted flickers of lightning.

An hour later they ran into a rainstorm. The storm increased. Several hours later the train ground to a halt. A trestle across Old Hat Creek had gone out, the conductor explained. They spent the evening there while the cattle bawled and fretted. Then it was learned that the trestle could not be repaired for several days. The cattle would be turned out and held beside the track. A freight outfit was passing and the passengers could ride back to Bellfontaine if they wished. Allie was one of those that returned.

It was shortly after dawn when she arrived in Bellfontaine. Every bone in her body ached from the hours in the jolting bed of a half-empty freight wagon. Her portmanteau was still on the train. When she had had a good sleep she would go to Si Gorman's and buy herself a dress.

After walking to the white house she removed her shoes

and entered. There was no use in waking Paul at this early hour. She could explain her return later.

She was tiptoeing to her room when Paul said suddenly from his bedroom, "Who's out there?"

"It's me—Allie."

She thought she heard voices in Paul's room. Then the door opened and he put his head out. Sleep was heavy in his eyes. She told him about the washed-out trestle. He seemed very upset.

"Why don't you go to the hotel?" he demanded.

His tone angered her. "Why should I? My money paid the rent on this house."

He looked back into the bedroom, biting his lip. Then he said thinly, "All right, so now you know."

"Know what?"

Without answering he went back into the room and slammed shut the door. Allie sank wearily to a chair in the parlor. In a few moments Paul came out wearing his black suit. He was belligerent.

"You came back to spy on me," he shouted.

"I have no interest in what you do," she said. Then she nodded toward his room. "Who's in there?"

He stiffened and did not look at her. "I'm going to the hotel for my breakfast." He went to the front door, then turned, flushing slightly. "You might make Margretha some coffee."

When he had gone Allie went into the kitchen and built a fire. She had the coffee boiling by the time Margretha entered. She was pale and pretty and seemed only faintly embarrassed when their eyes met. "I suppose you'll tell Carse," she said.

Allie shook her head. She poured coffee into two cups and put them on the table. They sipped the coffee in silence.

Margretha wiped her lips daintily on a napkin. She had long gloves in her lap, and as she drew them on she said, "Your brother and I—"

"My half brother," Allie corrected.

"All right, your half brother. He and I are business partners in a way."

Allie gave her a hard smile across the table. "A unique way to transact business."

Margretha finished drawing on her gloves. She wore a green dress of some stiff material. "Paul said you'd likely not understand. He suggested I try to convince you not to let this become a source of gossip."

"Paul's good at that. Running away and leaving someone else to face up to what he's done."

"We—we didn't expect you back."

"Naturally." She leaned across the table. "You lied about Carse Boling."

Margretha's gray eyes were frightened. "No."

"You change your affections easily."

"I'm in love with Paul. Is that a crime?"

Allie searched the pretty, vapid face. "Not if you're sincere, which I doubt. Now tell me about Carse."

"I—I thought I loved him. At the time."

Suddenly Allie reached across the table and caught Margretha by a gloved hand. "That day at the river. You and Carse. It never happened, did it? Not the way you told it. And the doctor. It was just a game you decided to play."

Margretha got to her feet and tried to pry Allie's fingers from her hand. "Let go of me!" she cried, a note of panic in her voice.

Allie rose and swung Margretha against the wall so hard that a lock of pale hair fell across the girl's forehead. "Tell me the truth."

They wrestled across the kitchen. Margretha tried to reach the coffeepot, but Allie slapped her hard across the face. Margretha began to weep.

After a moment she said, "It was a lie," and tears poured through the gloved fingers she pressed to her eyes.

Sickened, Allie left the house. She got a room at the hotel and stayed there the rest of the day.

At noon Carse, Stag, and Emily were in the jail office telling their story to Sheriff Luke Alcorte. When they had finished, the Sheriff vigorously blew his nose in a bandanna. "This is the damnedest thing I ever heard of." He looked hard at Staggart. "You sure you wasn't drunk the day of the shooting, and that maybe—"

"I was cold sober," Stag said. "I never killed Luz, if that's what you're thinkin'."

"Just want to be sure," Alcorte said, and scratched his head. "What do we do now?"

"We'll get a lawyer, Luke," Emily said.

"There's none in town except Grover Penn. And he's

just a river lawyer. And the circuit judge ain't due for a month."

"They're not going to hang my husband for something he didn't do." Emily's black eyes were bright with determination. "You remember that, Luke."

Alcorte swore softly. "So it was Kellerway that spread them stories about you and Carse. A man that low ain't fit to breathe the same air as decent people."

Emily gave Stag a tight smile. "It'll work out."

Staggart was staring through the barred window of the jail office, his face loose and gray. "I hope so." He put a hand to his throat. "Hangin' is no way for a man to die. I'd rather shoot myself."

Sheriff Alcorte took a ring of keys from the wall. "If we're goin' to be legal all the way through, I'll have to lock you up, Stag. I hate to do it, but—"

"Get word to New Mexico," Stag said fiercely. "The sooner it's over, the better I'll like it."

Later, Emily stood outside the door of her husband's cell. "I understand a lot of things now, Stag. Why you'd go to Min's once a year and drink yourself into a stupor. But I wish you'd told me the reason." She put a small hand through the bars. "It would have been better for me to help you than some strange woman."

"I wish I could believe that, Em."

"You gave me a home, you gave Johnny"—her voice broke—"a job."

"I wish I could do it over," Stag said with an anguished cry. "Maybe Johnny would still be alive."

"One thing we learn, Stag. We can never do anything over."

"Why don't you hate me, Em? I'm weak—yellow."

"We settled that last night. You're my husband and I'm your wife. Whatever burdens you have I'll share."

"But you don't love me. You never have. Not really."

"As I told Carse," Emily said soberly, "I don't really know what love is. Maybe nobody does. Maybe love is standing by the person you share your life with. Maybe it's working together, building. If there's more to it, I'll learn, Stag. When this is over we'll go away for a time."

He gripped the bars. "What if the law in New Mexico won't give me another trial?"

"They'll never hang you. Bet on that with everything you have."

The news that Staggart was held in jail on an old murder charge stunned the town. Those that liked him said it was impossible that he had shot a woman. That he had also been accused of killing his partner, Elmo Hoyt, was of little importance. It was the death of the woman that counted. Those that hated all successful men had a different idea. They said that probably Staggart's greed caused him to commit murder so as to obtain the silver mine his partner had found. Stag's friends visited him in jail and brought him cigars and food and whisky. The whisky he stubbornly refused, and this surprised them.

The day of Staggart's voluntary imprisonment, Paul Kellerway was at the edge of town where the Coffin herd, which he had forced Staggart to sign over to him, was bedded down. Unaware of Staggart's latest move, he had ridden out with Charlie Granson, buyer for the Archer packing house, to look over the cattle.

Granson, a heavy-set man in a checked suit, sat the saddle of a pinto and let his practiced eye run over the beef in the Coffin brand. Kellerway wore a brown suit and his hat was set at a jaunty angle on his dark hair. He smoked a cheroot and studied Granson from the saddle of a sleek black gelding.

Granson peered down at a legal-looking paper he held in the hand that rested on the saddle horn. It stated that ownership in 2,500 head of Coffin cows was transferred to Paul Kellerway.

Granson looked skeptical. It was Staggart's signature on the document, all right. "Why would Stag turn that much over to you?"

Kellerway was very businesslike. "He owed me some money. It's his way of paying off." Kellerway felt a mounting tension as he saw Granson again study the assignment. The stiff breeze whipping across the flats from the river disturbed the ends of the string tie that lay across the snowy bosom of Kellerway's shirt. "I'd like to deal with you," he told Granson, "but frankly, some of your competitors are interested."

It was Granson's job to buy good beef for his packing house at the cheapest possible price. Yet one thing puzzled him about this deal. "Carse Boling is Staggart's partner, but his signature doesn't appear on this document."

Kellerway pointed out that Staggart owned a controlling interest in Coffin. But Granson still hedged, stating that to be legal the transfer should bear both of the signatures.

"Staggart and Carse Boling have worked this out between themselves," Kellerway said. Behind him an engine clanked onto a siding with a string of empty cattle cars. "I intend to stay permanently in this country, Granson. What if I could guarantee you so many head a year at a good price?"

Granson was not so easily taken in. "Explain yourself," he said.

"Aside from this Coffin herd, I also hold options on the herds that four of the small outfits intend to ship."

Granson was blunt. "I'm not sure I like your methods. You come to town and set yourself up as a representative of a nonexistent packing house. And you do that in order to get options from these small ranchers, selling them on some ridiculous theory of pooling their interests."

Kellerway smiled archly. "You're a businessman and so am I. It isn't the method that counts in the long run, but results." He paused dramatically, then said, "To cement our friendship for future deals, I'll let you have the Coffin herd for five dollars a head under market price."

Granson kept surprise from showing on his face as he swiftly calculated that this reduction in price would amount to a saving of well over twelve thousand dollars. "I'm used to haggling over price," he said, "but this is quite a cut."

Kellerway saw he had captured Granson's interest. "To play fair with your company you can't afford to turn this down."

"No, I suppose not." Granson studied the handsome face a moment. "I must have a guarantee of clear title to this herd."

"You'll get it. And when we conclude this transaction we'll talk about the options I hold on the other herds."

"Kellerway, you're an ambitious man."

Paul Kellerway's mouth hardened. He wanted to say: I've found my niche at last. Nobody is going to dislodge me from it. "I am ambitious," he confessed. "Next year when you return, I might have my own saloon. And my own sheriff." He added significantly, "The Radich brothers and I could possibly control this country."

Granson could not help showing his surprise. "I've been angling for their business for years. But—"

"Deal with me and you might sign a contract with the Radich boys. I say *might*. You never know."

After his talk with Alcorte and seeing Stag locked up, Carse decided to rectify one of Stag's many mistakes. No longer was there any reason to fear Kellerway. The matter of the business in New Mexico was in the open at last. Therefore, he decided to see if the Coffin herd had yet been sold. At Goodfellow's he learned that Kellerway had left a half hour before with Granson.

Riding swiftly to the east end of town, where loading pens stretched along the tracks, Carse Boling arrived at the holding ground just as Granson made up his mind to buy. The cattle buyer was about to return the assignment to Kellerway when he saw the tall, grim figure of the Coffin partner skirt the herd on a dun horse. Carse nodded to Charlie Granson, and saw the quick apprehension in Kellerway's yellow-brown eyes, directed at the paper the buyer held in his hand. Carse rode his dun between the mounts of the two men just as Kellerway reached for the paper.

"I'll take that paper, Charlie," Carse said, and snatched it from Granson's hand. Kellerway was forced to rein in his spirited black. Some of Kellerway's pickup crew, holding the herd, looked on uncertainly at the man's cry of rage. Kellerway rammed a hand beneath his black coat, but Carse sent the dun horse at a hard run, causing the black to rear. As Carse flashed by he clubbed Kellerway with a fist on the back of the neck. Kellerway and the revolver he had tried to draw went flying into the dust. The black horse careened toward the herd and one of the hands caught it up.

Carse drew his revolver and gave the crew a hard look. "How about it, boys?" he asked quietly. "Did Kellerway pay you to watch this herd, or to fight for it?"

The men exchanged glances as the herd stirred restlessly behind them. A bony, tobacco-chewing rider said, "We ain't drawed fightin' pay, that's for sure."

"Then keep out of it," Carse said. "You'll get five dollars apiece from me if you stick till the herd is sold." Then he shifted his glance to Kellerway, who had picked himself up and was striding toward the revolver that lay half buried in the dust.

"Hold it," Carse warned, and Kellerway turned, staring at the .45 Carse held. "It would suit me to finish it here and now," Carse went on. "For your half sister's sake, I won't put a bullet in your head." He cocked the weapon. "But don't tempt me. Your day here is done. Clear out."

Slowly Kellerway brushed off his clothing. "Let me tell you something, Boling," he said with a savage smile. "Because of your interference here today I'm going to see that Staggart is hanged by the neck until he's dead."

Charlie Granson uttered a startled cry at this news, but Carse continued to stare at Kellerway with no emotion on his dark features. Kellerway looked uneasy at Carse's lack of surprise, but he plunged on: "Now give me that assignment or I'll go to the Sheriff. The herd is legally mine, and if you persist in this attitude I'll have you arrested for rustling."

Then Carse told him that the story of the murders in New Mexico was all over town; that Stag had allowed Alcorte to lock him up. Carse tore the assignment into small pieces. "Your blackmail didn't work," he said.

Kellerway crossed the bed ground, boarded his black horse, and rode it at a hard gallop back to town.

Charlie Granson slowly let the air out of his lungs. "So it was blackmail."

Carse told him the details of the shootings back in New Mexico. "Charlie, I know Kellerway probably made you a cheap price for this herd. We've done business with you for years, and it's been a fair shake on both sides. How about coming down to the jail and getting together with Staggart? The three of us can work out a deal."

"Good enough," Granson said. Then he rubbed his chin worriedly. "Do you think Staggart can get out of this mess he's in?"

"Emily wants to do it legally. I'll play it her way—for now."

As they rode to the jail, Granson said, "What's this talk about Kellerway's tie-in with the Radich brothers?"

Carse laughed. "So that's the bait he used." Then he sobered. "Bert Radich will play with Kellerway only as long as he thinks the man will be of some use."

Granson frowned. "It's amazing how a man like Kellerway can come into a country and get himself a stake with his crooked methods. Do you know he's optioned the herds of some little outfits hereabouts? And that the fools can't sell until Kellerway gives his consent?"

"I tried to warn Ralph Shamley," Carse said. "But, Charlie, if you call them fools, you're putting yourself in the same saddle. After all, Kellerway nearly had you sold."

"I'm afraid he did," Granson admitted.

Chapter Twenty-one

PAUL KELLERWAY dismissed the fact that Staggart had decided to fight at this late date as one of the hazards of the hard game he was playing. After leaving his horse at Ekert's he walked toward Goodfellow's. The back of his neck pained where Carse Boling's fist had struck him.

Several times he was stopped by men who were anxious to discuss the startling news that Staggart, the second biggest rancher in the territory, was accused of murdering his old partner and a Mexican woman. Kellerway expressed the opinion that a man who'd kill a woman should be strung up immediately without bothering the authorities in New Mexico. But no one seemed to be fired up enough to carry out his suggestion of lynching, so he let the idea drop.

In Goodfellow's he found Bert Radich at the bar. He bought the rancher a drink and commented on Staggart's predicament. "Must be a shock to you, Bert, to learn after all these years that your neighbor shot down a woman in cold blood."

"Nothing shocks me," Bert Radich said through his beard. "I hear Carse Boling grabbed the herd Stag turned over to you."

Kellerway's face flamed and he rubbed the back of his sore neck. Of course, there had been witnesses to the scene at the bed grounds, and he knew the word had quickly spread. Men in the saloon were looking his way, and he knew they were waiting to see how he would get back at Boling.

"I'd have control of Coffin by this time, Bert," he said, forcing the rage from his voice, "but for Boling."

"Well, it was a nice try. Thanks for the drink."

Kellerway turned white as Radich turned away. The rancher had made it plain that he was not going to help. "You said you'd be interested in Coffin if I could get a controlling interest," Kellerway snapped softly.

"But you ain't got it." Radich looked at him. "If you do, then come around for a talk."

"I have an ace up my sleeve," Kellerway said, and managed a conspiratorial smile. He was thankful he'd had the foresight to cultivate the vain, pretty woman who was Staggart's niece.

"It'll have to be a big ace," Radich said, interest flickering in his eyes. "You haven't had much luck with Boling. Lopart and Quince died for their trouble." Radich added, "And you'll need more than Sam Jedrow to finish the job."

"You might know the names of a couple of tough boys," Kellerway suggested quietly.

Bert Radich brushed the back of a hand over his curling beard. "It's your fight. Not mine."

Kellerway went to Merle Lanniman's ferry, for it had been pointed out to him that the old ferryman was a source of information. It cost him twenty dollars to open negotiations.

"This pair are ex-railroad detectives," Lanniman said confidentially. "They busted up a train-robbing gang last spring, and they didn't take any live prisoners. But they don't work cheap."

"What are their names?" Kellerway asked.

Lanniman gave him a shrewd glance and started to cast off his ferry. "I disremember," he said, but his memory cleared when Kellerway, cursing softly, dropped another gold piece into the outstretched hand. "Monty Coomb and Chick Barrett. They're holed up in a shack at the end of Ferris Street." When Kellerway started away, curiosity got the better of the old man. "Who you figure to send these fellas after?"

Feeling reckless, Kellerway said, "Carse Boling."

Lanniman's face paled. "Golly, if I'd knowed that, I wouldn't have talked."

Kellerway, giving him a hard smile, stepped off the ferry. "Don't be afraid of Carse Boling. Nobody lives forever."

Later, in his office, Kellerway wrote a long letter to the authorities in Mogollon, New Mexico.

In conclusion he wrote: "As the two chief prosecution witnesses, Sam Jedrow and myself will gladly return to New Mexico to attend any hearing pertaining to the matter. We still feel strongly over the cold-blooded murder of the Mexican woman and her common-law husband. This man should be executed as soon as possible to satisfy the needs of justice. Yours, Paul J. Kellerway."

After mailing the letter at the wicket in Si Gorman's store, Kellerway set out on another important mission. He found Margretha at Ekert's, about to hire a man to drive her to Coffin.

Kellerway swept off his hat and kissed her gloved hand. "I don't want you to go to the ranch. Stay with me."

Her face reddened. "Allie was hardly cordial," Margretha snapped.

"You can't blame her, I suppose. How was she to know I intended to ask for your hand in marriage?"

Margretha, frowning, stared up at him. Then she smiled into his handsome face and took his arm.

Because Emily wished to stay at the hotel in town, so that she could visit Stag daily at the jail, Carse returned to Coffin in order to handle the endless details of a ranch of that size. One of the five-year hands, Red Dolman, he made *segundo*. It was a post that should have been filled years ago, but Stag had stubbornly put off doing anything about it. Once Stag had rashly promised the job to Johnny D'Orr, but his dislike of Emily's brother had made him reluctant to keep his promise. And then Sam Jedrow had come along and held the job temporarily. Now Jedrow was fired and Johnny D'Orr was dead. No matter how this business might turn out, Carse thought one night in his quarters, there were things Stag had done that would be hard to forgive.

Again he wondered if he should try to stay at Coffin or go back to Texas, as he had planned. There seemed to be nothing to hold him here. Allie, he had heard indirectly, had left town. And he and Emily had proved beyond doubt that there was nothing to their friendship but just that—friendship. But he also realized that Staggart was fundamentally weak, and if the man escaped the harsh justice a New Mexican jury had voted for him, there were still the Radich brothers waiting to crowd in from the north. No, a man had obligations. He would stay and see it through with Stag and Emily. Perhaps one day he could buy a half interest in the place. Of one thing he was certain: He would not marry Stag's niece to gain that advantage, no matter how much his partner might wish it.

He was supervising the breaking of some horses one noon three weeks after Stag's imprisonment when Allie Kellerway rode into the yard. Because of the cooling weather, she wore a leather jacket over her shirt. She swung down, her face grave.

Despite himself, Carse felt his pulse leap at sight of the clear brown eyes in the lovely face. "I heard you left the country," he said, trying to be casual about it.

She explained about the washed-out trestle. "I'm glad I came back. It gave me a chance to learn that Margretha lied about you."

"I tried to tell you," Carse said stiffly, and watched a funnel of dust rise above the breaking corral.

"She and Paul were married two weeks ago."

"Two of a kind," Carse snapped, and sensed that this would present new problems to Coffin.

"I didn't come here to argue," Allie said. "I—I just want you to know I'm desperately sorry for the way things have turned out for your partner. Emily is a brave woman."

Apprehension tightened his mouth. "There's been news from New Mexico?"

"Yes, this morning." Allie's face lost color. "I told Emily I would bring you the word. The authorities in New Mexico say they have letters from many people demanding that Staggart pay for his crime. They indicate they don't favor granting a new trial."

Carse swore softly. At best there would be months in jail for Stag in New Mexico while his lawyer attempted to save him; months for Emily burdened with worry. He crossed to his quarters, yelling at one of the hands to saddle a horse. He came out of the lean-to wearing his gun.

As he moved to the corral, Allie hurried after him. "Don't kill Paul. Please, whatever you do."

Roughly he said, "Why should it make any difference whether I do the job or somebody else? His kind is bound to end up on the wrong end of a gun."

She blocked him, standing with hands at her sides, lips parted in an attitude of surrender. "You should know why I asked you, Carse. You should know."

Her meaning was plain, and for an instant he forgot himself and reached for her. Then he said savagely, "It's no use, Allie. Once before you tried to get my promise to stay away from him."

Her eyes were misty. "I'm asking you again. I don't want his death to come between us. I—I'll do anything to keep you from killing Paul. Anything to persuade you that having me is preferable to the other."

For a long moment he was tempted; then he shook his

head. "Allie, it would be no good. You'd only be hurt in the long run, because I'd break my promise."

He mounted the horse that had been saddled. Her fingers reached for his hand. "Then let me warn you. Paul has hired two gunmen. They're tough and hard and cruel. I've seen their faces."

"You frighten me."

"Don't jest, please. It might mean your life." Her lips trembled. "Have you ever heard of Chick Barrett and Monty Coomb?"

"No," he told her, but it was a lie. He felt the short hairs stiffen at the back of his neck.

The long ride to Bellfontaine was made in silence. In Ekert's Livery she made one last plea. "I don't have much use for Paul. But as I told you before, we both had the same father. I could never come to you if he died by your hand."

She ran from the stable and he thought she was crying. He couldn't be sure.

Chapter Twenty-two

As Carse moved uptown from Ekert's he saw the change in Bellfontaine. Shipping was over. The Red Devil Dance Hall was closed. The walks were nearly deserted. A few of the extra hands still hung around, but with the first real blast of winter they would drift south. Overhead the sky was clear, but the sun had no warmth.

He met Ralph Shamley on the walk. Shamley looked whipped. "I should have taken your advice, Carse. Kellerway sold the herds for five dollars a head under market."

"What did you expect, Ralph? He had nothing to lose. He takes his profit and you boys are left holding."

Shamley said, "This about finishes me. I got the word that Bert Radich will make me an offer, so he can expand so much them government surveyors that're comin' in won't dare touch his land. I'll either take his bean money or go under."

Carse put a hand on Shamley's arm. "Coffin would rather you stayed in business. We'll see about a loan and worry about government surveyors later."

Shamley pursed his lips. "Talk around town today is that Stag ain't goin' to be in no position to make a loan. He's sure to hang, they say."

Carse said grimly, "Don't count a man out until they bury him."

He moved away from the dispirited Shamley and crossed to the Empire Hotel. He found Emily, plainly worried, on the veranda.

"I wonder if I did the right thing," she said, "trying to get Stag to clear his name." She beat a hand against the porch railing. "But it must be right, Carse. We can't have that awful charge hanging over his head the rest of our lives. He'll go out of his mind and I'll go out of mine."

"Em, don't give up," he said gently.

"Sometimes I curse this white blood of mine," she said, her voice shaking. "Why can't I be a full-blooded Oglala and butcher a beef at issue day? Eat raw liver dipped in the gall bladder and pour the blood into the cow's stomach and heat it with rocks from a campfire and drink it?"

"Stop it, Em."

"No worries but food, and pitching the tepee so the opening always points east to catch the first sun." She leaned against one of the overhead supports. "Sometimes this white man's life is too much for me, Carse."

"It's not like you to quit fighting," he said severely.

She looked up at him and her eyes were moist. "I know. I sound as bitter as Johnny used to."

"Em, you did what you thought was best for Stag. If things look black, I'll get him out of jail—one way or another. You and he can go to Canada. I'll run Coffin."

With a visible effort Emily got control of herself. She had been under a strain and the receipt of the letter from New Mexico had unnerved her temporarily.

"Maybe Stag won't wait for you to get him out of jail if things go wrong," Emily said. "He's like a crazy man since that letter came. Kellerway has stirred him up again, painting those horrible pictures of a man hanging."

"I'll have a talk with Kellerway," Carse promised.

"Stag was so sure the matter could be settled here, without having to go back to New Mexico. Frankly, I'm worried that he won't take his lawyer's advice and wait it out. At least until we can talk with the authorities."

He heard Emily's quick indrawn breath and turned to follow her gaze. Two men came along the walk, paused, and looked up at him on the veranda.

"Hello, Boling," Monty Coomb said, shifting a quill pick to the opposite side of his long mouth. He had steady, colorless eyes. "Haven't seen you since spring."

Carse felt Emily stiffen at his side. Monty Coomb wore his revolver jammed carelessly into the waistband of black-ribbed trousers. Chick Barrett, at his side, was shorter, stocky, and carried his gun in a holster ornate with silver.

"I hear you boys aren't working for the railroad any longer," Carse said thinly.

Coomb and Barrett exchanged tight glances. "We got a new job," Coomb said. He removed the quill pick from his mouth and spat into the street. "How about a little poker at Goodfellow's? Maybe tonight?"

"Maybe," Carse said, and watched Chick Barrett smile.

They waved to him and then crossed to Goodfellow's.

Emily shuddered. "They're working for Paul Kellerway." Her voice rose in anxiety. "Why can't the Sheriff arrest them? How can he be so blind as to allow these men to walk the streets, when they're here but for one purpose?"

"The Sheriff can't arrest them until they break the law," Carse pointed out.

"The law." Emily's lips curled. "Alcorte will jump if the Radich boys tell him to. Not before. Bert Radich wants to see Coomb and Barrett do their work."

"It might be more of a job than they figure."

"You've been lucky so far, Carse," Emily said, a faint agony in her voice. "How long can your luck hold?"

"Long enough."

His apparent indifference caused her dark eyes to widen against his tight face. "You realize what their job probably is? To kill you." He nodded absently, and she took him by the arms and shook him fiercely. "Carse, haven't you any feelings at all? My God, you discussed playing poker with them as if they were old friends and not two men who plan to murder you."

He felt a tautness in his stomach and was glad she did not sense what might be terror insidiously burgeoning through every fiber of his being. "Go down and cheer up Stag," he suggested.

"Carse, why can't you bring the crew to town and wipe out Kellerway and his hired killers? Is it any worse than to have them shoot you down?"

Carse shook his head. "The Radich brothers have made it plain that if I do that they'll step in. It'll mean a full-blown range war and a lot of men will die."

"But it will save your life."

"Not necessarily. I can't ask my men to face a thing like that. The Radich boys aren't fooling."

"And I thought they were good neighbors," she said.

"Em, operating a cattle ranch is the most cutthroat business in the world. It's the era for expansion. The shirttail crowd like Ralph Shamley can hardly hold out any longer. It's the day of the big operator. You can't blame the Radich boys for gambling on Kellerway." He sighed. "Maybe I'd do the same thing if the tables were turned."

The fading sun brought out the lights in Emily's dark hair as she gave a vigorous shake of her head. "Not you, Carse. You would never take advantage of a situation."

He was staring across the street at the window of Paul Kellerway's office. "Maybe I'm too soft. Maybe I've got no right to be in this country or in this business."

Emily's smile was gentle. "Carse, you're a good man.

This country will remember you a lot longer than it will Kellerway or the Radich brothers."

"You haven't read much history. It's the conquerors that get the honors."

Emily said, "Daddy used to tell of his own father, who fought with Napoleon. Daddy's father left France to get away from that sort of blood-letting. And here we have it in our own back yard. Kellerway and the Radich brothers."

"Em, you can't change the world. A lot of people have tried. All you can do is live your own life. If there ever is any changing, then it will come about so slowly that nobody will even notice."

As he started to leave, she said, "Carse, I pray this will end right for all of us. And if it does—" She broke off.

"Yes, Em?"

"Carse, you need a wife. Not a woman like me, or Margretha. Allie is—"

He cut her off with a lift of his hand. "Before this is over Paul Kellerway will die. Or I will. Either way, I'll be no earthly good to her."

He went down the steps and crossed the street, aware of a tension along his spine. The weight of the gun at his belt seemed somehow to be an ugly reminder of the only way this business could be settled. He saw men looking at him strangely and he knew that it was no secret that Kellerway had hired two men to kill him. He climbed the stairs to Kellerway's office and without knocking opened the door. Kellerway sat behind his flat-topped desk, studying some papers. Now he rose, his yellow-brown eyes hard.

"I hear you've been to see Staggart at the jail," Carse said coldly. "Been building up his fear of hanging."

Kellerway came around the desk and leaned against it. He wore his black suit and white shirt.

Carse said, "I'm surprised you didn't send Coomb and Barrett to Coffin to stalk me. Or maybe you thought they'd have the same bad luck as Lopart and Quince. Is this how you figured it? To wait until I came to town?"

"You're telling the story," Kellerway said. He took a cheroot from the desk, bit off the end. He put the cigar in his mouth but did not light it.

Carse closed the door and stepped to one side and put his back to the wall. "By the way, how much did you get out of that mine Stag's partner found in New Mexico?"

Kellerway gave him a hard smile. "So you know about

that. Elmo Hoyt was a braggart. There wasn't five hundred dollars' worth of silver."

"But you thought he had made a strike. And you followed him to camp and killed him and the woman."

Kellerway came away from the desk, tall, slender, compact. "If you intend to pursue this possibility, let me remind you of the facts. Stag killed them, not I. As I testified at the trial, Staggart was trying to dispose of the bodies when I arrived. And remember this." Kellerway's voice sharpened. "He's a convicted murderer who escaped from jail the day he was to die. The carrying out of his execution will be a mere formality in the eyes of the law."

"There'll be a new trial."

Kellerway shook his head. "It's eleven years since the trial. Some who might have spoken a good word for Staggart are dead or have moved away. But the two prosecution witnesses will go before a judge in New Mexico and say Staggart should hang. And the two witnesses are Jedrow and myself. There isn't one person alive who can swear he didn't kill Hoyt and the woman. Only Staggart's word against ours." Kellerway, satisfied with himself, leaned back against the desk again.

Carse said, "You've been planning this a long time."

Kellerway shrugged. "It was mere luck that I happened to be in Chicago last fall when Staggart came in with a shipment of Coffin beef. He'd changed, but I thought I recognized him. Jedrow and I made inquiries."

"You made your plans for nothing."

Kellerway smiled wisely. "You and the Mrs. Staggart you found so charming the night Sam Jedrow caught you together in the woods should be happy Staggart will be eliminated from your lives."

Carse said, "I didn't think Jedrow would talk about that."

"It was a slip when he told me, I'll admit," Kellerway said easily. "He and I had some arguments over my plan to pit you and Staggart against his wife. But Jedrow was enraged that he had misjudged the woman. He thought her to be noble."

Carse said, "I doubt if Jedrow will tell anyone else— Stag, for instance. That is, if you're trying to pressure Stag again with the same tactics."

"Jedrow's a fool sometimes, but he'll do what I say."

"Maybe not where Emily Staggart is concerned."

"Don't bank on it," Kellerway said. "A long time ago Jedrow had a wife. Her name was Lydia. She looked a lot like Emily Staggart. It's Jedrow's only soft spot." Kellerway's gaze thinned. "He hated you before, but his hate is double now after learning the truth about you and the Staggart woman. It's become an obsession with him to kill you." Kellerway laughed quietly. "You whipped him with your fists, I'll give you credit for that. But you'll never beat him with a gun."

"If you're so sure, why did you hire Coomb and Barrett?"

Kellerway shrugged. "Just insuring the bet."

"Jedrow killed Johnny D'Orr. And Lopart, a man you hired, killed a kid by mistake. You'll pay for that, Kellerway."

Kellerway looked uneasy. "Get out of here, Boling. I'm expecting my wife and I don't want to upset her."

"Do you think with Margretha for a wife you'll have another lever against Coffin?"

"As you know, she's Staggart's only kin."

"You're forgetting Emily."

"I'll deal with Staggart's widow. With Margretha I have, shall we say, better cards in my hand." Kellerway got a look of impatience on his face. "I don't understand your purpose in all this questioning, but I've had enough."

"The purpose was to decide whether to kill you now and get it over with," Carse said, and saw that Kellerway's forehead was suddenly beaded with sweat. "You've probably got a gun under your coat. Why don't you reach for it?"

"You're a fool, Boling," Kellerway said with an attempt at his old jaunty air. "You should know that to win you never give the other man a chance to beat you."

"You're already beaten."

Kellerway's eyes were a little wild. "I've gambled everything on this, Boling. I'm not going to stand by and see you ruin it. It's my one last chance to get a stake."

"Funny, but Art Quince told me the same thing the night I killed him." Carse jerked open the door. He went out into the hall and down the stairs to the street.

It was dark now and he went down the street and took his evening meal at the German Café. On the wall was a cheap lithograph of "The Last Supper." He wondered if it was somehow prophetic.

Chapter Twenty-three

KELLERWAY FOUND Coomb and Barrett in Goodfellow's. He cautioned them about getting drunk. It was the supper hour and Goodfellow's was almost deserted. "Boling's pretty tough," Coomb said, chewing on his quill pick. "Me and Chick don't think we're bein' paid enough."

Kellerway checked his quick rage. "I intend taking over Coffin. I'll need a foreman and a *segundo*. Men I can trust." When he saw no softening of Coomb's hard features, he added, "Of course, there will be a share in the profits."

The chunky Barrett said, "Won't be no jobs for us if you sell out to the Radich brothers, like we hear you aim to. Providing you get hold of Coffin."

"Maybe I've changed my mind," Kellerway said with a trace of anger as he recalled Bert Radich's refusal to help him. "With a strong enough crew I could tell them to go to hell."

"Reckon you could, at that," Coomb agreed. "Guess we might get Carse Boling in a poker game, yell 'cheat,' and blow him out of his pants."

"You'll have to be more subtle than that," Kellerway warned. "But Boling can come later. First, there's Staggart. Since that letter came from New Mexico this morning he's convinced he'll hang. And I've paid him a visit and helped with the convincing."

"Did you sneak a gun to him?" Barrett asked quietly.

"I had it done. When the waiter carried in his tray tonight there was a gun under the napkin. The waiter convinced Staggart the gun was from a friend and that this friend would have a saddled horse waiting after nine tonight."

"You think he's pressured enough to try to make a break?" Coomb wanted to know.

"You be there and find out," Kellerway said. "After that you can take care of the matter of Carse Boling."

Then he went to the Empire Hotel. Two representatives of the Acme Packing House, Kansas City, had arrived on the afternoon train. They had heard that Kellerway was a man with beef connections and they wanted to discuss business. If Kellerway could corner the beef market here, as he had led them to believe by his letters, then they would sign a contract. Their names were Emerson and Bates. They were well-dressed, cigar-smoking men. Kellerway met them in the lobby.

"We might have some relaxation before our business," Kellerway suggested. "Good food, fine wine, and everything else that makes an evening worth while. I tell you, there's probably nothing in Kansas City any better than Big Min's."

Carl Emerson, who had a boyish face framed by prematurely gray hair, winked at Bates. "I've heard of the place."

"I'll call for you here at eight o'clock," Kellerway said, and they shook hands.

"Quite a fellow," Emerson said as Kellerway left. "You know, if he's everything he claims, we'll give the Chicago buyers a run for their money."

"You know what they say about counting chickens," Bates said realistically.

As Kellerway was crossing the veranda, he met Emily Staggart on the steps. A really handsome woman, he thought, and for a moment he was touched with shame at the memory of his vicious attacks upon her name. He tipped his hat and she gave him such a cold stare that he felt a shiver along his spine. He went along the walk into the darkness, feeling a sudden depression. Was it worth it? he asked himself. He had alienated his half sister and the small ranchers thoroughly hated him. Then he stiffened his back. Anything was worth it, he vowed as he continued toward the house he now shared with Margretha.

After his supper Carse Boling looked through the lamp-lighted windows of Goodfellow's and saw Coomb and Barrett at the bar. He entered and saw that the pair had spotted him in the backbar mirror. Chick Barrett let a hand fall casually to the butt of the revolver in the silver-trimmed holster. But the lank Coomb nudged him and gave a slight shake of his head.

Carse exchanged greetings with several tight-faced men at the bar. Carelessly he took a position about three feet from Coomb and Barrett. He spoke to them. There was an unnatural quiet in the saloon and Carse knew that trouble was expected now that he was standing beside the men everyone knew had been hired to kill him. But the tension eased when Carse talked to Oren Goodfellow about the need for rain and the possibilities of the beef market for next year. Coomb and Barrett exchanged glances, shrugged, and continued with their drinking.

Bert Radich came in from the privy behind the saloon and took his seat in the poker game he had temporarily left. The bearded rancher lifted a glass and said, "Luck, Carse."

Carse turned easily, smiling. "Luck for what, Bert?"

Bert Radich let his gaze slide to the backs of Coomb and Barrett at the bar, then he turned his attention to his cards.

The doors banged open suddenly and old Ben Smiley hobbled in. Under a thin arm he carried Staggart's old Sharps rifle.

Carse Boling's gaze thinned. "Who told you to come to town?" he said gruffly.

"Nobody," Ben Smiley said. He sounded half drunk. "I ain't workin' for Coffin no more," the old cook went on loudly.

"And you've taken Stag's rifle instead of wages?" Carse asked quietly.

"Maybe," Ben Smiley snapped. He took a quick drink, then turned and glared across the room at Bert Radich. "I'm through at Coffin. Maybe you can use a cook, Radich."

Radich thoughtfully fingered his curling beard. "You haven't quit Coffin, old man," he said.

"The hell I haven't."

Carse caught the old man by an arm. "I appreciate your trying to help me, Ben."

Smiley shook off Carse's hand. "I'm helpin' myself. Nobody else."

Carse smiled thinly. "And you don't have to make Bert Radich think you've quit Coffin. So if you get in a fight he won't think I'm getting help from the Coffin crew."

They had spoken quietly. The old cook glared at Carse. "You better change your brand of whisky. You sure are loco." He hobbled out, swearing, the big rifle tucked under his arm.

"Tough old man," Chick Barrett commented.

Carse saw that Oren Goodfellow's face was pale and his

eyes were worried. "Oren, give me a bottle of that Aquarius water Johnny used to drink."

Goodfellow blinked in astonishment. "I never knew you to drink anything but whisky."

"It seems sort of fitting to drink Johnny's Aquarius water, seeing as how I intend to settle up for him."

There was a hush in the barroom and men craned their necks to see what was going on. Carse took the bottle Goodfellow passed across the bar. He faced Coomb and Barrett, who stood beside him, looking uncertain.

"Luck, boys," Carse said. But instead of drinking, he lashed out with the bottle at the nearest man. Coomb was hit in the center of his lean face. Blood spurted from a cheek laid open and Coomb yelled and lurched against Barrett, who belatedly was trying to draw his gun. Carse swung again and the end of the bottle caught Barrett a glancing blow on the forehead sufficient to knock him to the floor. Barrett, cursing, rolled aside, but Carse jammed his foot down hard on the silvered holster, pinning Barrett's thick fingers to the gun grip. Barrett screamed.

Stepping back, Carse drew his gun. Coomb had an elbow on the bar, trying to hold himself erect. Blood poured across the left side of his face. He seemed dazed. Barrett had come to a sitting position on the floor, shaking his bruised fingers. His eyes were murderous.

Bert Radich had got to his feet at the poker table. There was a grudging admiration in his eyes. "Guess I wasted my time wishing you luck. You had it all the time."

Goodfellow said, "Lock 'em up, Carse! In jail!"

Carse shook his head. He was looking at Radich. "We've got a political sheriff, who always worries which side of the fence he should be on. Oren, have you got a good stout storeroom where we can store these boys?"

Goodfellow, smiling, led the way down a hall. Carse herded Coomb and Barrett into a small room with a barred window. "Tell Kellerway you didn't earn your money," Carse said to the pair.

Barrett hugged his injured fingers. "Finishing you will be a job I'll be glad to do for free."

Carse slammed shut the heavy door and fastened it with a padlock. His knees were shaking. Then he left by the rear door and stepped out into the thick Dakota night. He went to the veranda of the Empire House and settled down in the shadows to watch the street that led to Paul Kellerway's house.

It had started, he told himself, and the thing must irrevocably be settled this night. His luck, such as it was, might not hold another twenty-four hours.

The depression stayed with Paul Kellerway as he changed his clothes. He could hear Margretha stirring about in the front part of the house. It had come as a surprise to learn that she was helpless in the kitchen. That meant he would have to hire a woman to do the cooking. But he had postponed doing anything about it, for he needed every dollar. Things had gone badly because of Carse Boling. But this time he was confident of success. He'd had to pay Coomb and Barrett five hundred dollars and this had strapped him.

As he surveyed his handsome face in the mirror he considered his position objectively. It had seemed so simple to put the fear of God in Staggart and pressure him into turning over the Coffin herd he intended to ship. Perhaps he had been too greedy, he told himself, in not stopping there. But it had seemed incongruous not to pursue the possibilities further. He had demanded of Staggart a quarter interest in Coffin in payment for his silence on the New Mexico matter. Once this was obtained, he had felt sure he could obtain control of the ranch.

But now Carse Boling had forced him to give up the herd and Staggart was in jail. He damned Jedrow's softness where Emily Staggart was concerned. Jedrow should have finished Boling that night he caught him with the woman, and to hell with the fact that she was looking on.

He was doggedly determined to be a success here. And those that had been cold to him would suffer. Goodfellow, for instance, and Si Gorman. A new saloon and a general store would give them rough competition.

Margretha came to the bedroom, frowning when she saw he wore his best suit. "Since we've been married we've only eaten at the hotel once. I'm sick of the German Café. Can't we go to the hotel tonight?"

"I'm busy." He brushed his dark hair. He told her about the men from the packing house.

Her eyes brightened and she fussed with her pale hair. "Why couldn't we entertain them here? We could get a woman to cook and another to serve."

"This is business," he snapped, "not social."

His tone angered her. "I thought by this time we'd be living at Coffin." He was tying his tie and did not answer her. "Things would have been different if I'd married Carse Boling."

"He didn't want you."

Her lips curled. "I could have had him."

He laughed harshly. "You're my wife, so forget about Boling. He'll be eliminated very shortly."

"You've brought in some men to kill him," she said. "The talk is all over town."

He shrugged and buckled on his shoulder sling. Then he examined the loads in his revolver and dropped it into the holster. He found that the palms of his hands were sweating.

"I don't think I trust you, Paul," Margretha said.

"It's too late to do anything about that now."

"I could divorce you."

"And give up your chance for Coffin?"

"I shouldn't have listened to you. I could have married Carse and I'd own half the ranch just by being his wife. Uncle Stag promised. It would be much better than being married to a man who doesn't love me."

He forced himself to embrace her and caress her with his hands. "I've got to entertain these two men tonight. There'll be some drinking at Goodfellow's, so don't expect me until you see me." He started for the door.

"Just don't let me hear of you going to Big Min's," she said shrilly. "You bring something home to me and—and I'll kill you."

Sam Jedrow was waiting for him in the parlor. Jedrow had been shot in the left shoulder the night he had jumped Carse and Emily, but he no longer carried his arm in a sling. He wore a suit that fitted his big frame snugly. His green eyes were hard and resentful.

"I don't like this keeping out of sight all the time," Jedrow complained bitterly.

Kellerway dropped a hand to his shoulder. "Well, it'll be over after tonight. I've got a business appointment tonight and I want you with me. That's why I sent word for you to meet me."

"Scared Boling might jump you?" Jedrow said thinly, and heaved himself out of the chair.

"I think we'll see the finish of him tonight. But I don't

want him climbing my back while I talk business in case something goes wrong."

He kissed Margretha lightly and saw her narrowed pale eyes watching him. He wondered if somehow he had underestimated her. He and Jedrow left the house and walked in the darkness toward town. He met Allie coming toward the house, and told Jedrow to go ahead and wait for him.

Allie said, "Paul, I'm asking you to stop this mad plan of yours."

"It's no mad plan," he said. "Can't you understand it's simply business?"

"Don't try to charm me, Paul. I know you and Jedrow have been blackmailing Staggart. You caused the death of Emily's brother and the Peavey boy. And now you want to see Carse Boling dead. You call that business."

"Allie, you'll get back your two thousand dollars. That's all that should concern you."

Suddenly from the pocket of the black cloak she wore Allie drew a small revolver. "Paul, I'm not going to let you do it."

He felt shaken to see his own half sister holding a gun on him. The inside of his mouth felt dry. "Allie, don't meddle in something that doesn't concern you," he said sternly.

"Carse Boling concerns me very much. I love him. And I don't want him to kill you. I'll do it myself, if it must be done."

So intent was she on Paul that she did not see Jedrow come up behind her. A thick arm went about her waist and the revolver was torn from her grasp and hurled into the street.

Jedrow stepped back and Kellerway said, "Thanks, Sam." He felt sweat on the back of his shirt.

There was a sudden gunshot from another part of town. The three of them stood in the darkness a moment, and then a man rocketing by on horseback yelled: "Staggart's escaped. He shot the Sheriff!"

Kellerway felt a thin elation and Allie cried, "You planned this, Paul! You—you're not fit to live!" She turned and ran up the street and he saw her merge with the crowd now streaming in the direction of the jail.

Chapter Twenty-four

THAT MORNING when Stag first heard the grim news from Sheriff Alcorte he felt that it was the end of his world. Representatives of the law were going to arrive and take him back to New Mexico. They would be right behind the letter that had arrived. Maybe tomorrow. Emily had tried to cheer him up, but to no avail.

Now at full dark he restlessly paced his cell. He had refused his supper, but the gun the waiter had smuggled in was hidden under his mattress. He did not know who this friend might be that had given him a gun and offered to have a horse outside. But he couldn't wait until nine o'clock for the horse to be there. He was hot and cold alternately and he felt very ill.

He took the gun from its hiding place and with a trembling hand put it into his belt and buttoned his shirt over it. Today Kellerway had come here and told a revolting story of Sam Jedrow's finding Emily and Carse in camp together the night they had run away. Carse had never told him of this. And Kellerway had indicated that Emily and Carse were going to let him hang so they could be together.

He didn't want to believe this, but his mind was in such a turmoil that there was no logic to his thinking.

Terror gripped him as he called the Sheriff's name. In a moment Alcorte came along the corridor, carrying a lamp. The Sheriff was gray and drawn as he peered in at Staggart, sitting on the edge of the cot.

"Stag, I'm damn sorry that things look so black for you. If it'd been me, I think I'd have lit out for Canada."

"Luke, come in here and talk to me."

The Sheriff put the lamp on a shelf, hesitated a moment, then said, "We can talk through the bars."

"Hell, Luke, you act like you're afraid of me."

Alcorte rubbed perspiring hands along his pants. "All right, I'll do it," he said, as if making up his mind to some momentous decision.

He unlocked the door and entered the cell and stood with his back to the stone wall. "I want you to know, Stag, that I don't think you killed them people. And I don't want to see you hang. I ain't much of a sheriff. Too scared, I reckon. I let the Radich boys push me too much."

Staggart did not hear him. There was a great roaring in his ears. He suddenly leaped to his feet, jerking the gun from under his shirt with such violence that the hammer caught briefly on a fold of cloth. There was an explosion and Sheriff Alcorte sank to the floor.

Stunned, the rancher looked down at this man who had been his friend and who was now looking up at him out of eyes dull from bullet shock. "Luke, I—"

"My God, Stag, you didn't have to shoot me. I was goin' to let you out and claim you escaped. I seen the gun the waiter had hid under the napkin. You didn't have to shoot me."

The Sheriff groaned and rolled over on his face, his arms loose.

"Oh, God," Staggart said, with the reverberations of the gunshot still crashing in his ears.

Completely panicked, he rushed out into the darkness. There was no saddled horse nearby. Already he could hear shouts from the main street, and the sound of men running toward the jail. He cut across a vacant lot and skirted some shacks. And as he ran blindly he knew he had completely ruined Emily's life by this rash act. And he knew he was a moral coward, not fit for her love. Maybe she and Carse would be better off without him, at that.

And then as he reached Chicago Street he saw four men coming along the walk. Paul Kellerway was talking amiably to two men in white shirts, smoking cigars. Behind them stalked the giant Sam Jedrow.

"Let's not let this unpleasantness spoil our evening, gentlemen," Kellerway was saying. "They'll run Staggart down soon enough." The men entered Big Min's and the door closed behind them.

At the sound of the shot Carse had left the veranda of the hotel and sprinted toward the jail. He felt cold when he heard the grim news from a man on horseback. Then, from a corner of his eye, he saw Kellerway and three men moving along the walk. He knew Stag was beyond all help now. Grimly he followed the men.

Later, Carse went to the back door of Min's and knocked softly. In a moment the door opened and he saw, framed in lamplight, the enormous figure of the woman. Carse shouldered his way into a narrow hall.

"I heard about Stag," Min said. "It's awful."

"Min, get your girls out of here."

Min stared at him. "You're after Kellerway?" He nodded. "If he caused Stag to do this, I'm sorry I didn't poison him." She opened some doors and said in a quiet commanding voice, "Pearl, Louise, Helen. Get out the back door. There's going to be trouble."

Carse heard the squealing girls, caught the scent of perfume. White bare shoulders, black-clad legs fled past him and into the night. Then he went along the hall past a small kitchen. He heard piano music and stepped into the parlor.

Kellerway sat with two strangers at a table covered with a white tablecloth. They were drinking wine, chatting casually. Sam Jedrow sat in a chair tipped back against the wall. The big face was scowling. Outside came the pound of hoofbeats as riders swept west along Chicago Street, probably in search of the fleeing Staggart.

A step behind him caused Carse to whirl. He saw Staggart, gaunt and perspiring, in the hall. Stag held a revolver. He looked ill, but he managed a wan smile.

"Didn't think I had the guts to side you when it came to a showdown?" the rancher said, and brushed past Carse and into the parlor.

Carse tried to grab him, for Stag was spoiling the element of surprise he had counted on. But it was too late. Kellerway cried, "Staggart!"

Sam Jedrow lurched to his feet, kicking over his chair. Kellerway had a hand beneath his coat. The two cattle buyers got out of their chairs. In his haste Emerson spilled wine all over the front of his shirt.

"Get out of here," Carse told them.

The two men rushed for the front door. The frantic yellow-haired Lew jumped off his piano stool just as Kellerway drew and fired. Carse tried for him and the bullet crashed into the piano keys, setting up a discordant jangle of notes. Bits of ivory flew into Kellerway's face and he flung up an arm to shield his eyes. The ivory cut his left cheek. Jedrow's heavy gun had swung up and the crashing of guns was deafening. Emerson and Bates had run to the street, leaving the door wide open.

Jedrow fell back, a dazed look on his big face, as Carse

found the range. Staggart emptied his gun into Paul Keller-way and the man fell loosely across the table, upsetting the wine bottle as his fingers clawed at the tablecloth.

Carse tried to lift his gun to finish Jedrow, but there was no strength left in his arm and he realized he had been hit. He shifted the gun, but by this time Jedrow had crashed headfirst through the side window.

From outside came the sudden blast of a rifle and old Ben Smiley's shout: "Watch it, Carse! Coomb and Bar-rett! Bert Radich turned 'em loose!"

The heavy gun spoke again and a man screamed. Carse lurched onto the porch of Big Min's and saw Chick Bar-rett sprawled in the center of the street. Monty Coomb stood with hands raised. Old Ben Smiley had discarded the Sharps for a revolver, and its muzzle was pressed against Coomb's back.

"Where's Jedrow?" Carse cried, and realized his voice was unsteady. The street seemed to swim before his eyes.

"Across the street. He's holed up!" Ben Smiley flung out a hand, indicating a dark, deserted building that once had housed a land company. The front door stood open.

Stag came up behind Carse. "I'll get him. It's my fight."

A shot came from the building and Carse butted Stag off balance with his shoulder as the bullet screamed into an upstairs window of Big Min's.

Men were converging on the area, and Carse saw Emily. She was screaming at him above the tumult. And he saw Sheriff Luke Alcorte carried by two men who had made a chair of their hands. The Sheriff was white in the glow of lanterns carried by some of the crowd. There was a thick bloody bandage on his right thigh and his trouser leg had been cut away.

Staggart stood as if stunned; he was staring at the Sher-iff, and Luke Alcorte said weakly, "It's all right, Stag. I ain't bad hurt."

Carse started lurching across the street, but Emily grabbed him. "You've been hit, Carse!"

He tried to push her away. "I'm going after Jedrow."

"No, Carse!" she cried.

Ben Smiley, who still held his gun on Coomb, said, "I think Jedrow's about done. You got him in the stomach. He was bleedin' bad when he come out of Min's."

Some of the men shouted, "We'll all go after Jedrow!"

Carse broke away from Emily and put his gun on them. "There's been enough killing. Johnny and the Peavey kid. And it's my fault, a lot of it. I should have spoken up when Jedrow first came to Coffin. I should have made Stag face up—" His head was reeling again.

Emily had run to Big Min, who stood on her porch, and then Min had ducked into her place and come out with pencil and paper. Taking these, Emily started across the street to the deserted building while the crowd watched her silently. Carse blocked her.

"Carse, you've tried your way. Now I'm trying mine. Don't try to stop me." She lifted her voice. "Jedrow, this is Emily Staggart. Can you hear me?"

After a moment there was a weak answer: "Yeah, I hear you."

"I'm coming in," Emily Staggart said, and she walked resolutely into the darkened building at the moment Carse's legs went out from under him and he fell to the street.

He awakened to find that he had been dragged to the walk and that his head lay in a soft lap. He looked up and Allie's face swam above him.

"Emily," he said suddenly, and tried to sit up.

"Lie still," Allie commanded. "You've got a broken collarbone."

At that moment Emily came out of the building. "He's dead," she told the crowd. Then she crossed to the Sheriff and handed him a piece of paper.

He still sat on the seat made by the hands of two men. He read the paper and looked at Emily. "This paper," he said as loud as he could, "clears Staggart. It says that Paul Kellerway and Jedrow killed Elmo Hoyt and the Mexican woman." The Sheriff's voice began to shake as he looked at the dazed Staggart. "You're free, Stag. When them fellas come from New Mexico, we got something to show 'em, boy."

They got Carse moved to the hotel. Stag was in the room, and Emily and Allie Kellerway. Stag kept saying over and over, "But it's a lie, Emily. They didn't do the killin'. It happened just like I said."

Emily looked at her stricken husband. "Is it a lie when it will save the life of my husband?" she said.

"But how—how did you get him to admit this?" Staggart said, shaking his head in disbelief.

"He was dying and he knew it," Emily said. "I asked him to do one decent thing. And he did." She put a hand to her eyes. "Just before he died he called me Lydia. I wonder . . ."

"His wife," Carse said from the bed. "Kellerway told me Jedrow had one soft spot. I guess he was right."

Bert Radich and his brother crowded into the room and Carse regarded them coolly.

"This is it, Bert," Carse said, holding tightly to Allie's hand. "Kellerway is dead. So is Jedrow."

Bert Radich fingered his curling beard. "I told you I was waitin' to see which side won. Yours won, so that's how it is."

"We'll be watching you, Bert. Remember that."

"You can't blame me for trying. Hell, you'd have done the same thing."

"Maybe. I don't honestly know."

"Well, we're still neighbors," Bert Radich said. "Might be a good idea for us to get along. There's new fellas movin' in all the time. Maybe next time there's trouble we oughta make it a point to be on the same side of the fence."

"We'll see, Bert. We'll see."

Ardo Radich said, "You're our neighbor, like Bert says. And Bert's right. He sure is right."

When they had left, Emily said, "Stag, you offered Carse a half interest if he married your niece. You can do the same if he marries Allie. He's earned it, Stag. Without his help you'd have nothing."

"Without him I'd be dead." He fingered his throat.

Carse did not protest. He felt numb, except for the throbbing pain at his collarbone. "What about Margretha?" he asked.

"She's gone," Emily said. "I told her to let us know where she'll be. I want to send her some money. Despite what she's done, she's Stag's kin. And"—her voice broke— "I was almost a widow myself. I know how she must feel about it."

They went out and Allie knelt beside the bed. "I'd have come to you, Carse. Even if you'd killed Paul."

"But I didn't."

"I know. Stag did." The brown eyes were gentle on his face. "I'm burying Paul tomorrow, Carse. I don't feel too badly. I remember him when I was a little girl. I liked him then. But he was too ambitious. I guess that's all you can say about him."

"You heard what Stag offered me?" he said.

"Yes. But you haven't asked me to marry you." She smiled. "I'll wait a decent length of time after I bury Paul. A month, say. Shall we be married then, Carse?"

His head nodded on the pillow. "We'll build a house, Allie. We'll live at Coffin, but we'll lead our own lives, and let Stag and Emily live theirs."

Against the windowpane fell the first flake of winter snow, and he found he did not long for Texas at all.

THE END